# Stellarnauts

William Allen

# Dedication

I would like to dedicate this book to my mom, Ruby Allen. She has been my biggest supporter. From the first time I mentioned writing a book, me a 40-year-old construction worker telling his mother that he wanted to write a book. What does she do? From the very beginning believed in and supported me.

I love you mom, thank you for everything!

# Content

## Part 1

## Part 2

## Part 3

# Part 1

# Chapter 1

Zorath

6227 ASST

The rocky surface of the steep incline baked in the fierce glow of the red sun at Lena's back as she stepped onto the uppermost stone. The rocks were searing from such exposure to the sky's oppressive rays that, by the time she was only a few feet into her ascent, they had the young girl praising herself for remembering to bring the insulated climbing gloves and some knee guards this time around. She patted the ruddy dust off her hands and onto her tan cargo shorts. She then wiped her brow and looked skyward to acknowledge the time. There was still more than half a day left before it was dark, and she would need to return home.

She surveyed the vast landscape below her and noticed a steep hillside to the east that she had missed on the way up. She noted it as a potential footpath to reach the mountaintop again later before turning around to continue her trek. The top of the mountain was mostly flat for nearly a mile in the direction Lena was going before it came to another incline. Luckily, it was not nearly as steep as what she had just spent her morning scaling. With her gear fastened securely in place, she made her way across the plateau to continue her venture. She needed to complete as much exploration to the north as possible before nightfall, knowing that her parents would expect her home before the sun dipped below the horizon.

As she trotted along the surface, she had made it about halfway to the next stone's face before her boots came to a halt. She had nearly passed right by it, but something caught her eye as she walked. Right in the center of the mountaintop, barely visible from even a few feet away, there was a slight opening that led downward into the body of the mountain. Lena stood there for a moment, glancing between the cave entrance and up the face of the mountainside. She was torn between two simple options: up or down.

After just a few moments of contemplation, she decided that today would be a good day for cave diving. With no chance of rain all week, she thought she could explore further up the mountain on another day, possibly a cooler one. The cave promised much-needed cooler temperatures. She dropped her climbing gear once more and peered down into the opening of the cave. It was more than wide enough to fit her petite body into, even with additional equipment on. After observing the area surrounding the entrance and planning her descent, Lena reached inside her backpack and pulled out the Ion lamp she often used to navigate Zorath's nighttime terrain when her father would bring her with him during his own outdoor activities. She had a feeling that she would need it today. Thus, she patted herself on the back once more. She was beginning to like the north.

She adjusted the lamp to produce a torch beam and then shone the light down into the blackness. Now, she could clearly see that there was just a small drop into the opening before reaching the cave floor. It was far enough down for her to jump in, let alone for her rope to easily reach. She had expected the depth to be greater and was honestly a bit disappointed that it wasn't.

Regardless, she pulled out the length of rope she had tucked inside her bag and tied it to a large stone that jutted up from the ground just a few feet from the cave. Once she had the rope secured, she put her backpack over her shoulders, fastened her lamp forward, set the timer on her wristband, and lowered herself into the cave. She only had to lower herself once before she reached the floor, nearly crashing into it.

After detaching her rope, she tested the depth again and found that she could stretch on her tiptoes, reaching the top rim of the cave with her fingertips, almost touching the outside. The length of the rope seemed kind of pathetic as she looked back at it, and it nearly gave Lena a first-person sense of embarrassment. However, the girl knew well to follow the safety precautions that she had been taught. Always and without exception. Besides, the rope would make it easier to get out, anyway.

Turning, the light of her lamp beaming out in front of her, she started down the narrow tunnel. As she pushed forward, Lena began to feel that something was off. She looked around, trying to put her finger on what was triggering her instinct when she realized. The natural walls of the cave had changed in such a subtle progression that Lena had not noticed until now. The walls, once coarse and bumpy, were now much smoother than Lena thought possible compared to all the other natural stones she had seen on Zorath. She rubbed her hands down them as she walked. Besides a layer of natural accumulation from the cave system, they were actually completely smooth—just as they seemed. It was uncanny and fascinating all at once. They seemed artificial, cut, and constructed with precision rather than shaped by the chaotic natural forces, Lena thought as she walked. The further she delved, the cave began to take on a more labyrinthine nature. There were a few spots where the strange corridor-like tunnels would split and go all in different directions.

When she came across this, Lena took out a bright, yellow-green glow marker and drew an arrow pointing in the direction from which she had come. It wasn't the proper method of marking, but it would have to do for now. Getting lost in a cave system was something that Lena's father had taught her to prevent at a young age. He, too, had a sense of exploration when he was younger, and his teachings made Lena a far better explorer than she would have been if he hadn't been the explorer that he was. That's why he joined the Stellarnaut Armada back before she was born; his sense of adventure put him on that path.

She checked her wristband multiple times while traversing further into the cave, and the deeper she went, the more frequently she would glance down at it. Not having the sun overhead or any other natural signs around made it difficult to know when to begin heading home. But each time she glanced at her wrist, there was always plenty of time remaining. Hence, she ventured deeper into the cave, possibilities about her discovery racing through her head.

Theories from a long-lost Zorathian civilization to her being in a psy-spore-induced dream wrestled for attention in her mind and excited her curiosity. Finally, she rounded a corner, and the cave opened up into an enormous cavern—so jarringly abyssal that it gave Lena a start to be suddenly pulled from the claustrophobic tunnels she had just grown accustomed to. She unfastened and held out her lamp to see how far into the darkness her beam could penetrate. To her surprise, the walls began reflecting the light in several places, bright and lustrous, beginning to illuminate the cavern before her. "Silver?" Her soft voice echoed across the chamber.

Once she was close enough to see what was being reflected, Lena's eyes widened. She turned and ran down each corridor, breaking around each turn. She ran until she made it to the first arrow that she drew, pointing toward the exit. Her boots faintly squealed as she slid to a stop on the cool, moist cave floor. Leaning her arm against the wall, right beside the arrow, she panted as her adrenaline began to plummet. As she started to regain her composure, Lena turned her head and ear toward the tunnel to see if she could hear movement. Listening for a moment, she began to question whether or not she had seen anything at all. She was so close to her greatest exploration yet, and she had let her nerves convince her to turn tail at the first truly fascinating thing this cave had to offer. "I'm so stupid," she kicked herself inside. "There's nothing there. It was just my imagination."

Lena forced herself to turn and walk back down the corridors toward the large open room where she saw it. Stepping back into the cavernous space, she, this time, approached where the light reflected. Peering intently at the strange, reflective area, she found, to her dismay and intrigue, that her mind did not fool her. There was a face, after all—a pale, resting face—on the other side of a small circular piece of glass, inside some sort of tomb-like mound of stone. In fact, as Lena glanced around, she saw that there were several of these mounds along the walls.

Reaching into her bag, Lena produced a small hammer and began tapping around where the glass was, careful not to hit it. She wanted to see if the stone would chip away to reveal anything, perhaps even more glass. Ultimately, though, she wanted to see if this face had a body. She wasn't completely convinced it was a real face because it looked metallic. She suspected that it was just some kind of idol, just as artificial as the rest of this place.

As she worked on the stone with focused taps, a small chunk fell away to reveal a metal surface underneath. This heightened Lena's interest. Tapping the metal with her hammer produced a tinkling sound and a buzz as the steel vibrated from the small amount of force. Putting the hammer away, she rubbed her hand against the metal and noticed how smooth it was, even more so than the stone of the strange cave walls. It was as if this metal device were brand new, completely untouched by the world. Turning her hammer, she started trying to drive the flat end between the stone and metal. This proved to be the best method for removing the stone from the metal that she could come up with. After what seemed like hours, Lena's arm was starting to feel a little wobbly. Her efforts weren't for naught, however. Lena observed, with confused fascination, at what she had unearthed. An entire metallic door, heavy like something industrial, with just a small circular window. And behind that window was still the strange face.

After a few moments of observation, Lena finally grabbed the handle of the door and took in a deep breath, trying to convince herself that this wasn't a bad idea. She pulled down on the handle, but nothing happened. The handle didn't move, and the door remained shut. After a few more tugs, she gave up and decided to explore the room further. Her investigation revealed multiple windows with metallic faces within the other mounds of stone.

"Have I stumbled upon someone's lost robotics lab? Or perhaps a long-lost alien species?" Lena wondered as she examined each of the windows around the room. She shone her beam around, and for the first time, she gathered an idea about the spatial shape of the room she was in. It was round with a high, domed ceiling. The ceiling itself was clear of any stone, like the strange devices, and was as shiny as a finely polished wheel from one of the vehicles in her father's shop.

Oh no, she thought, looking at her wristband. I'm going to be late. She gathered her belongings and headed for the exit. Once Lena made her way back to the surface, using the rope to aid herself in climbing out, she could tell that the sun was dipping below the horizon. She knew she wouldn't be home before the sunset and would have to hear about it from her mother. Her father understood losing time while exploring, but her mother did not. She could be ruthless when it came to thinking the worst immediately. Lena untied her rope from the stone and rolled it up. Late or not, I'm not leaving any gear behind like this. If someone came across it and either stole or, worse, went inside the cave and tampered with whatever was down there, I'd never get over it. I'm going to be in trouble either way, she thought.

It was nearly an hour after sunset when Lena finally made it home. She walked through the front door of the house her mother and father had moved to when they found out her mother was pregnant with her. It wasn't the grandest home in Zorath, but it had everything they needed and loved. Lena and her little brother each had a room of their own on the second floor, and there was more than enough living space on the first.

Once through the door, she took her habitual glance at the photo atop the picture shelf in the living room—the one of her father in his younger years, posing stoically for his graduation headshot from Stellarnauts Academy. She had seen it countless times in her short life, often admiring how brave and unmovable her father appeared in his brand-new suit, the discipline of his training etched across his expression, and the pride in his dark green eyes. It was a moment of immense accomplishment frozen in time; his now bearded and aged face was clean and youthful. His recently graying hair, once dark and short—flat on the top and shaved on the sides—was the hair of a youthful military man. The only thing that hadn't changed since this snapshot of time's past was the look in his eyes and the man behind them. Even though he looked different from how she knew him now, Lena always recognized the Stellarnaut in the photo as her daddy. It had become an unconscious habit to glance back at this photo every time she went inside, like her own private daily ritual that even she had stopped noticing herself doing.

She went straight to the washroom to clean up for dinner. Her father was sitting at the table, enjoying a mouthful of what looked to be ground beef and pasta. His eyes rolled up toward hers, and he shrugged a little as she passed him. Lena stepped into the hallway and made her way toward the washroom.

Lena's mother walked out of her room with Kian at her side. "Le Le!" Kian shouted with excitement in his voice. "You're home. Did you find me something today?" he asked.

"No, not this time, little brother," Lena replied to the lively boy.

"That's okay," he said, his flush red cheeks highlighted by the bright red Roboshark shirt that Lena's mother had him dressed in. "I'm just glad you're home. Mum's been worried to death." He ran over to Lena, wrapped his arms around her legs, and squeezed. Then, he looked back towards his mother. "I told you she was okay, Mum."

Lena couldn't help but look down and smile at her little brother, even though she knew she was just mere moments away from getting an earful from her mother. He was always so happy when she came back, and she could tell. The excitement seemed to always radiate from this young child, and she often found it delightfully contagious. Lena's eyes went back to her mother, who, in stark contrast, was glaring at her. "You know the rules, Lena," her mother said. "It's an hour past sunset, and you're just now getting in."

"I know, Mother. I'm sorry," Lena submitted, her expression sinking.

"Eria," her father's gentle voice came from the dinner table. "Be easy on the girl; it's not as if she does this regularly. She hasn't been out past dark since she was a little girl."

"I know, Darian," Eria called back, still looking at Lena with a hint of irritation in her tone. "I'm just so worried that she's going to get lost or hurt."

"I'm going to be fine, Mother," Lena reassured. "I always take more equipment than I'll ever need. Plus, I carry the first aid box you made for me every time I go out."

Eria eyed the teenager for a moment. "Very well," she finally said. "But if you're late again, you won't go back out exploring until you're eighteen, young lady."

"What?" Lena exclaimed. "That's nearly two years."

"Lena," her father spoke up again, a little more sternly than before. "Your Mother has spoken. Don't argue with her."

"Sorry, Daddy," she said, looking at him from the entry of the hallway. There was an undeniable shame in Lena's eyes. Her mother's scorn was bad enough, but one thing Lena could not bear was her father's disapproval. She turned to her mother and apologized, "I'm sorry, Mother. I won't let it happen again."

Lena and her family sat down that evening and enjoyed each other's company over dinner. She told them about the cave she found. However, she didn't utter a single word about the strange walls, metallic doors, or the robot faces she saw down there. Not a word.

The next morning, Lena awoke in her room to warm rays from the deep red sunrise on the horizon. They shined like lines through the blinds of her bedroom window and onto her waking face. She shielded her eyes with her pillow before the early morning light, and the songs of local fauna prompted her to rise. She got to her feet and then breezed through her morning routine. It was while she was cleaning her teeth that she decided that she would visit her father in his shop.

She stepped out the front door and was met with Zorath's warm morning air. She looked at the building that sat only a few hundred feet away, connected to her family's home by a gravel pathway. As she approached, she noticed that there were already various tools and parts in front of the small, hangar-like workshop that weren't there last night. Lena had come into this shop more times than she could ever hope to recollect, but she knew that in each memory she had, there was always something slightly different about how it looked inside. Her father stayed busy breaking down, repairing, improving, and rebuilding all manner of vehicles here. The resulting clutter often left the shop in what her father would call an "organized mess," which he would navigate as if he had an inventory ledger and that he would have completely cleaned by the end of his projects. He had a peculiar sense of his space in that way, in how he effortlessly could sort his tools in an efficient manner for the series of tasks he had to perform and also clean while he went; the result was like a coastal wave of vehicular paraphernalia, drowning the garage in a flood before clearing up just as quickly as it had come. Lena contributed to cleaning one, or two, or twenty things throughout the years. The "organized mess" allowed her to poke around for items that caught her interest, and if they were in any kind of excess, they would find their way into the small plastic storage bin underneath her bed.

She walked through the large, open door to the workshop, stepping underneath the huge sign above it that had manually applied lettering that read: "Zoravic's Shop." She could hear the whine of power tools and the hiss of sparks saturating the hard floor. Her father was already under the hood of a one-pilot ship she knew to be an early model Stinger Class fighter ship. The ship had a sleek design for quick strikes in high-speed dogfights. It had a narrow, arrowhead-shaped profile, giving it exceptional speed and maneuverability. It was the coolest thing Lena had ever seen, at least until her father's next project rolled through these shop doors.

She approached to ask if she could borrow one of his power supply packs and some small tools. On top of the tools and parts around, his shop was full of old spacecraft. A few belonged to him, but most were those he had been hired to repair. Her father was a pretty good pilot if what she had been told throughout her life was true. Although Lena had never seen him fly much herself, other than a few quick test flights around their land after he repaired a ship for customers, of which he had an unending patronage. It was well known that Darian Zoravic was the single best spacecraft mechanic in all of Zorath, perhaps even in the sector. Because of this, Lena's father got a lot of business from local pilots, not to mention the business he got from off-planet. Many exotic ships and engines from distant worlds made their first foray into the world of Zorath because of Darian's work. Systems never before seen, let alone touched, by any Zorathian in history could be found in this workshop. That was because Lena's daddy was the best, and everyone knew it, especially her.

"Of course," Darian said when she asked. He was just climbing out from underneath the hood of the Stinger. "Just make sure you grab one with a full charge. Wouldn't want you to get out and about and not have what you need." He walked over to the shelf where he stored his supply packs and battery chargers. Reaching under the bottom of the workstation there, he pulled out a small, lightweight power pack. "Here we are." He passed it to his daughter. "This one has a good charge and won't be too heavy if you're planning on climbing back up to your cave. There should be a small toolbox over there full of small wrenches and screwdrivers. It's the one I normally keep in the house. You can take it; just don't lose any of the stuff in it. Also, bring some subterranean gear this time. I don't want to have to go spelunking in order to find you later."

"Thank you," Lena replied, buttering her father with a big hug and a peck on his cheek. "Have you looked at the rear engine yet? I see you're still up in the belly where the front engine is located. Those early model Stingers are known for throwing out the rear fusion thrusters," she said. She knew he had more than likely already looked at all possibilities, but she always liked to make him think she knew what she was talking about when she would come into his shop. She liked to think that she had inherited some of her father's talent, so she would regularly try to display this to him. She hoped to make him proud, and though she couldn't always tell with him, it always did. Not the bits of trivia or her sharing his interest, though Darian did love that about her; it was her mind and her heart that did it. If there's one thing Darian knew about his Lena, it was that the girl knew how to try. She shared his curiosity and his overflowing industrious drive, and that resulted in her always learning new things. She always kept her eyes, ears, and mind wide open, whether it came to objects or to people. Darian loved her for it as well. Nothing in this world made the man more proud than Lena.

"Not yet, sweetheart, but I'll keep that in mind. Jahn said the front engine seemed to be losing power," he replied with a tone of thoughtful consideration as he climbed back into the belly of the Stinger. Lena chuckled and slung the power supply over her shoulders, right over the top of her backpack. "Have you flown it yet?" she asked as she picked up the small toolbox and headed out the door.

"Not yet," her father said from under the hood of the ship. Starlighter was sprayed on the side of it, just on the other side of where Darian was speaking loudly. It was the name the pilot, Jahn, apparently, had given his ship. It was nothing new for Darian Zoravic to have a ship with a name like that painted on the side of it in his shop, especially one from off-planet. Most locals didn't do much more than fly up to the local Planetary Bazaar to buy or sell goods, so they didn't see much point in wasting time naming their ship. Almost every ship had a serial number and was scanned in that way, anyway. "I'll probably take it out later if I can't figure out what's wrong soon. Be careful, baby girl."

"I will, Daddy," She replied, continuing her stride outside. "See you this evening."

Lena didn't waste any time getting back to the cave entrance. The sooner she arrived, the longer she would have to try and figure out how to get the door open. She wasn't sure how long these robot things had been buried there, but she figured her power supply pack should be more than enough to charge a lab that was clearly so ancient. She organized the plan of action in her thoughts as she scaled the steep incline of a footpath that she noticed during her exploit yesterday morning, reaching the top much quicker this time.

Once she made it to the cave, she pulled the rope from her backpack and tied it to the same stone as yesterday. She lowered herself in; once on the floor, she retrieved her lamp and powered it on. Just as she started to head down the walkway, she heard, "Lena." It was a small voice, soft and familiar. She stopped and looked around, "Kian?" she said, confused. "Is that you?"

"Lena, help me down." She looked up to the opening in the ceiling from where she had just come. Kian was up there, staring down at her. He must have been lying on the ground, the way his head looked as if it were just sticking straight out above her.

"What are you doing here?" she asked him, astonished at what she was seeing. Maybe there are psy-spores down here, after all, she thought for just a moment.

"I wanted to come with you," he said. "Can you please help me down? I want to see the cave."

Not wanting to waste half the day taking him back home, Lena agreed to come back up and help him down. She tied a loop in the rope and had him put his foot in it. Once he was ready, she lowered him down while he was standing in the loop. Luckily for her, he was still a very light little boy; most six-year-olds were almost too heavy to be picked up, let alone lowered into a cave. Kian was very thin and still small, making the process rather leisurely. To Lena, with her constant activity keeping her fit and strong, he might as well have been a big feather.

Once he was on the floor, she climbed back down and retrieved her lamp again, ready to go. "Kian," she said sternly. "You can't tell anyone about what you see here, okay?"

He held out his hand, fist clenched tightly, all but his little finger. "I pinky promise Lena."

She hooked her little finger over his, and she knew from that moment he would die before he told anyone what he saw in this cave. They ventured down through the cave, and all her markings from the day before were still there. She even made more on her way out so she would know exactly how to get back to where the large room with the devices was.

"Okay, Kian, here's where we're going," she instructed her little brother. He resembled some sort of small pup, standing there and looking up at her with all the excitement that a six-year-old generates when faced with the prospect of adventure. His eyes were opened wide, the blue in them glistening from the light of the lamp. He smiled at her widely, teeth showing both top and bottom rows, all but the one he lost a few days back. It hadn't started growing back in yet. "There are some things in here you've never seen before. Don't get scared; nothing's going to hurt you."

"Okay, let's go in. I want to see," he said. His little body was shaking with excitement as they walked in. Lena walked him over to the first window she saw, the one she cleared the stone away from. She set the lamp down and lifted him up so he could see into the window. His eyes went even wider than they were, and his bottom jaw dropped. After a few seconds of quiet, the young boy had to speak up. "A robot! Can we keep it?"

Lena just chuckled a bit and said, "We need to find out if it even works before we decide on anything like that." She went to work, unpacking the tools she brought and getting the power supply cables stretched out. Once she had everything out, she went to the door and started prying on the handle with a small pry bar from the toolbox.

Kian began digging around in the toolbox. He pulled out a screwdriver and went over to the door. He started taking screws out of what looked like a panel. He was having a difficult time at it, so Lena took the screwdriver, and she was almost shocked to find that the screwdriver he had selected fit the pattern of the panel bolts perfectly. It was an old screwdriver, but it made her realize that perhaps this whole cave was not as alien as it seemed. There was at least some connection between these devices and classic human construction. Maybe it was some leftover time capsule from one of a myriad of periods in galactic history. There was no telling from which period it could have come yet, though, and so Lena finished the work. Once all the screws were out, she removed the panel. Behind it were some wires, and she wasn't sure what to make of them because they were all the same color: black.

She traced her fingers down the wires, trying to see where each one led. After several minutes, she decided she knew which wires were the ones that went to the lock in the door. She hooked the power supply to the three wires, hoping she didn't have them backward. Once they were all connected to the power cables, she went over to the pack and put her finger on the switch. She told Kian to walk outside the room for a minute, took a few deep breaths, and then flipped the switch.

The door lit up, and so did the inside of the small room where the robot's face was. Lena stood and took a few steps backward, not taking her eyes off the door. The handle she had tried to turn popped out and turned to the right. Once that happened, the door slowly lifted away; she would have never guessed the door would have opened upward. Once the door was open, she could see the entire body of what she now confirmed had to be a robot that was hidden behind the door just a second before. There were large cables connected to its body, and they fell away with metallic clinks and hisses of released pressure after the door was completely opened.

Lena had moved no further back since the door started opening. But once the cables fell from the robot, the power that was being fed to the door started spreading throughout the large room in which Lena was standing. Small bolts of what appeared to be electrical discharge ran all through the room, from ceiling to floor, all of it surrounding Lena. Then, without warning, every last bit of it hit her right in the chest, drawn to her like some sort of power rod, and blasted her back against the stone wall of the room.

She lay there, slumped against the wall, for a few minutes before she got her bearings and started to rise. She looked up at the robot, its glowing, white eyes now opened. It began to move and started looking around. She jumped to her feet and ran from the room, grabbing Kian as she passed him and carried him to the last spot, where she drew the arrow leading in.

She turned and looked back towards the room as she held her brother in place by the shoulders. "Kian, you stay here," she said, not looking down at him. "I can't leave Dad's tools here; he told me not to lose them. I'll be right back."

"Okay, hurry up," he said. The little guy had no idea what they were running from as he wasn't inside the room when the robot's eyes opened, but he knew something big was happening. And it nearly had his little heart tunneling through his chest from pure excitement.

She started back down towards the room. After a few steps, she turned back again. "If I'm not back in a few minutes, get out of here. Go get Dad." Kian just nodded, peeking around the corner of the turn in the cave wall.

At the entrance to the large room, she put her back against the wall and slid towards the door in an attempt to sneak up before she looked inside. She wasn't very quiet as she scooted along the wall, but when she got there, she could see the robot had gotten out of the small device that it was in and was standing over the power supply pack. It seemed to be looking down at it. The thing either couldn't hear or hadn't heard her approach.

She tried to make her way around the opening and get over to the toolbox unnoticed. Once she got inside the room, a strange voice said, "Who…are…you?" The voice was slow, and the words were spread out. It was as if it had never spoken before and was trying to make sure it said the correct words. She froze, eyes opened wide and looking straight at the thing. It hadn't taken its eyes from the power supply. After she stood there quietly for a few more moments, its head lifted from where it had been staring this whole time and looked directly at her. "Who are you?" The voice came again, sounding just as confused with the dialogue, but the words came closer together as though it were understanding that the words it was saying were correct.

"Lena," was all she said.

"I am Arcturus," it said, then looked back down at the power supply pack

# Chapter 2

## Zorath 6227 ASST

"Is this what you used to awaken me?" Arcturus asked, pointing down at the power supply pack it had been observing.

Lena had already come to the conclusion that this 'Arcturus' was not a normal robot, maybe not even a robot at all. She stared at it as it observed the power supply pack. Its metallic outer shell was unlike any metal Lena had ever seen before. Without the obscurity of the glass covering, the details of its body were now clear for her to see. They gave Lena a sense of uncanniness that, after discovering his entombed face earlier, held no contest to. It appeared to be some sort of entity born from the fusion of the organic and the artificial. When it turned its head or moved its arms, its outer layer would shift as if it were human skin. The marble-esque face was emotive, resembling that of a person, yet cold and still robotic. However, the composition of this skin-like layer was clearly metallic, and it seemed as if not even a sledgehammer would dent it. "What are you?" Lena asked Arcturus, still not completely certain of what had happened or that it wasn't going to kill her.

"I am Biotan," Arcturus said, not looking back up at her. "You are human." It reached out toward the power supply, and a small bolt of electricity ran from its fingertip to it. "You could not have awakened me with this device. It is… dead," it said once the small bolt of energy made contact with the power supply pack.

Not understanding what she had just witnessed happen to the pack, Lena replied cautiously, "Well, no. It's dead now. It just needs to be recharged. I used all of its juice to power that door." She pointed towards the door that hung overhead. Arcturus looked at the door and then at Lena. "Why? Why did you use its power to awaken me?" he asked.

"I don't know…" She started when, in a flash of anxiety, she remembered Kian. She turned and ran to the opening leading out of the room. "Kian!" She yelled down the walkway.

"Lena," Kian's hesitant voice came from down the cave. "Is it safe?"

Not knowing the definite answer to that question, Lena simply replied, "I think so."

Kian came walking into the room a few seconds later. "Aww, that's cool," he said, looking at Arcturus. "You turned it on!"

"What is this?" Arcturus asked, pointing at Kian.

"That's Kian, my little brother," Lena answered.

"I've never seen a little human before," Arcturus said. "Is Kian…" It looked as though it were thinking. "A child?"

Lena looked at Arcturus, her head involuntarily tilting to the side a little. "You've never seen a child? And a human child at that?" she asked. "Who created you?"

"What do you mean?" Arcturus asked.

Lena took in a deep breath. "You're a robot," She started in a clinical, matter-of-fact tone. "A highly intelligent robot, but a robot all the same. Someone had to have created you."

Arcturus tilted its head as though to mimic Lena's display of confusion. "I was not created by something or someone. I was given life by my parents. Similar to the way humans are given life, but not altogether the same. You see, when two Biotans have a deep enough connection, they fuse their life force, and a new Biotan is born. Biotans are never children in the same sense as Kian is now. We never grow any larger than the day we are born. We are not born with pre-programmed knowledge like a creator-designed automaton, as you seem to assess me. We must learn, just as a human child does."

Lena tilted her head again while Kian just stared at Arcturus. "How old are you?" Kian asked Arcturus.

"I do not know," Arcturus answered. "If you could tell me the current date, I may be able to give you an accurate guess as to my age."

Kian bobbed his head a few times as if he were counting to himself. "I was born in 6221, so it's 6227 right now."

"6227?" Arcturus asked. "Is that the year of your planet or the year of human space-time?"

"ASST," Lena answered.

Arcturus turned its head in an urgent motion, almost in what Lena would describe as surprise. "It has only been a little over three thousand years?"

"Three thousand years?" Lena blurted out before she could stop herself. Realizing that she had already said something, she decided she would go ahead and ask. "You're telling me you're three thousand years old?"

"No," Arcturus said. "I never told you how old I am. Your little brother Kian asked, but I did not answer."

"You just said three thousand years," Lena said.

"I did say that; you are correct. However, I did not say that I was three thousand years old. My comment, 'It has only been three thousand years,' was an expression of how long we have been in cryo sleep. If we count the 2915 years that I have been in cryo sleep, then my age would be." It bobbed its head as if it were counting, picking up on Lena's and Kian's actions as if it were trying to fit in alongside them. "My sleep must have slowed my information processing for an undetermined temporary period. Yes, you were correct; I am slightly over three thousand years old."

"I wasn't correct," Lena said. "I was just saying the same thing you said."

"Either way," Arcturus started. "We must recharge your power pack. If we're to survive, we must awaken the rest of my people."

"We can't just awaken all your robot friends," Lena protested.

"Why not?" Kian asked. "He's pretty cool, Le Le. I think we should wake the rest of them up."

Arcturus looked at Kian, studying him, before turning back to Lena. "Yes, Le Le, I am pretty cool. It would be cool if you could awaken the rest of my people." Arcturus looked back at Kian and winked.

"Don't call me Le Le. Kian is the only one who calls me Le Le," Lena responded, glaring at Arcturus. "And you," she pointed at Kian, "can't be taking his side. At least not until we figure out what is going on." She started pacing around the larger room.

"Are you a boy or a girl robot?" Kian looked up at Arcturus and asked.

Arcturus looked down at the boy and tilted its head again, processing the question. "Are you inquiring about my equivalent to the common carbon-based sexes of organic fauna, determined through chromosome patterns classified as XX, often titled 'female,' and XY, often titled 'male,' but through the use of the alternative classifications 'boy' and 'girl'?" It asked.

"I dunno. You seem like a boy robot, though. Are you?"

Arcturus processed the question once more for a few seconds longer. "This is… acceptable." He then turned his attention back to Lena, watching her as she walked around the room. He was trying to figure out what she was doing, and the human child's questioning was slowing his assessment. After a minute or so, he finally asked, "What are you doing, Lena?"

"Thinking," she said. "I can't believe this happened." She looked at Arcturus as she stopped walking. "I'm going to be in so much trouble. Mother and father are going to kill me." Arcturus was visibly confused by this statement. He once again tilted his head at Lena.

"Your parents? These are your co-creators, correct?"

"Yes," Lena said, running her fingers through her hair. "They're not really going to kill me. It's just an expression. I'm saying I'm going to get into serious trouble."

Nodding, Arcturus said, "I believe I understand." He then stepped towards the power supply pack and bent over to pick it up. "Could we exit and get this power pack charged? So that we can power up the ship and awaken the rest of my people? We are going to need them if we are all to survive."

"Ship?" Lena questioned. "Are we in a ship?"

"Of course," Arcturus said. "The ship we currently stand in brought me and my people to this uninhabited planet to hide. Although, it does seem to be unable to be operated, even if we were to power it up, now that you mention it," he acknowledged as he looked around.

Lena felt like she was in a dream. This day went from simple exploration to now having a member of an unknown species standing here, talking to her, asking for help lest they all be doomed. *Psy-spores,* she thought again to herself before shaking her head. She looked up at Arcturus, still shaking her head, but this time as an answer, "No."

Arcturus turned to her. "Why not? Why can we not charge the power pack?"

Her expressions of denial growing more animated from frustration, Lena elaborated. "No, that's not what I meant. I mean, no, you can't go with us. You have to stay here. If you go walking around out there, people will freak out."

He walked over to her and handed her the power supply. "That is acceptable. I am putting all of the trust of my people's survival in your hands. Once we wake them, we must find a way to traverse from this planet. We will be hunted once more now that I have been awakened."

Feeling pressure from having that responsibility placed on her shoulders, Lena reached out to take the power supply. As she did, a tingling sensation began to grow in her arm, and then a small electrical surge shot from her fingertips towards the power supply pack, not unlike what Arcturus did a few minutes before. The yellow lights on the side of it lit up and then started blinking faster and faster until they just stopped. Then, the pack started smoking.

Arcturus dropped the pack and started waving his hands up and down to cool them off. "Are you okay?" Lena asked, concerned.

"I am," he replied. "The power pack overheated, I believe." Kian bent over to pick it up. "Kian, no," Lena said.

Arcturus stepped forward and nudged the pack out of Kian's reach with his foot. "The power pack is very hot, Kian. I would not advise picking it up just yet."

Lena looked up at Arcturus, a little taken by this gesture. "Thank you," she said, "You just saved my little brother from burning himself."

Arcturus tilted his head once again. "You are welcome. I would trust you to do the same if it were me or my..." He paused for a moment, then continued, "I do not have a little brother, so it does not make much sense to continue my thought process." He tilted his head again, trying to find the proper words to deliver his last message in a more effective manner. "You are aiding in the revival of my people, so I anticipate that you understand my sentiment."

Lena laughed. With all that had happened and as stressed as she was, she needed that laugh. Arcturus's way of communicating was so strange, and his stiff delivery was something she knew would take some getting used to. She walked over to and bent over the power supply pack. She held her hand over the top of it. She couldn't feel any more heat radiating from it, so she moved closer and tapped her fingers against its outer surface. The pack had cooled, so she picked it up and addressed her peculiar new acquaintance once again. "I'll return tomorrow with a charged pack. What do you intend to do while we're away?"

"If I could use your tool, I would like to clear away some of the... build up... around the chamber doors. This will make access easier when you return with a charged power pack."

Hesitantly, Lena set the toolbox her father had let her borrow on the ground at Arcturus's feet and stepped back. "You have to promise to keep them safe. They belong to my father, and he entrusted them to me."

Arcturus held up his right hand, and all of his digits spiraled together into an odd, twisted cyclone-like shape, his fingers twisting like metallic tentacle appendages. The faint light underneath his chest glowed brighter. Once he appeared like some otherworldly statue, he spoke. "You have my word as a Biotan and as an independent entity that no harm or damage will come to these tools while they are in my care."

Lena just nodded slowly and took Kian by the hand. "Come on, Kian, let's go. Tell Arcturus bye."

"Bye, Arcturus," Kian said excitedly. "We will see you tomorrow. Have a good night."

Arcturus apparently took this as an acceptance of his promise, and so his light faded, and his hand returned to normal. With that, Lena and Kian turned and walked from the cave, leaving Arcturus and her father's tools behind. She promised she wouldn't lose his tools, so she had to return, regardless.

Lena and Kian reached the cave entrance, and she checked to make sure the knot was still tight on the loop she tied in the rope for Kian. Once she was satisfied, he would be able to stand in it while she pulled him out; she pulled herself out first.

"Okay, Kian, put your foot in the loop and hang on to the rope while I pull you out," she said to him as she looked back down, taking the rope in hand. Kian complied and stepped into the loop, holding on to the rope. It was a lot harder lifting him out than it was lowering him into the cave, but once she got him out, they gathered what they needed and were on their way.

They returned home a short while later, and Lena went straight into her father's shop. He was standing on a small stepladder with his head under the side panel of the Starlighter, the same ship he was working on when they left.

"Hey, Daddy," Lena said when she walked in.

He took one step down and bent over so he could see under the ship. "Hey, sweetie, did Kian go with you today? There was a piece of parchment in the dining room that said, 'Went with Lena.' Your mother was concerned, but I told her he would be fine with you."

"Yeah, he already went to the house. Said he was hungry," she responded. "I didn't invite him along; he just took it upon himself to follow me. But it was fine; I enjoyed his company today. Moving forward, he'll need to let me know in advance so I can pack enough food for both of us."

Darian squinted his eyes suspiciously. "If you don't want him tagging along, sweetheart, we can make him stay home."

"No, it really was fine." Lena just wanted to get the power supply charged and go to her room. She had a book on all the alien species ever encountered by the Solianic civilization, whether from the many worlds of the **Intergalactic Star Fleet** or through outreach discoveries by the **Stellarnauts.** No matter how many times she read through the book, she couldn't recall ever seeing anything about a 'Biotan' alien species. "Where can I plug this power supply pack in?" she asked him.

He had already stepped back up into the ship's underbelly, and he replied, "Just put it over on the shelf I got it from this morning. I will plug it in later."

"Okay, can I use it again tomorrow?" she asked, hoping the thing still worked after it overheated the way it did.

"No problem," he said, never coming back down to see her plug the thing in.

Once she set the power supply pack on the shelf, she turned and left the shop, heading back to the house. Her mother was sitting at her desk in the office, working on some new model she and her partner were engineering.

Her mother looked up from the computer at Lena when she walked through the door. Without a word, she rose to her feet and walked straight to her daughter. Reaching inside her pocket, she pulled a piece of parchment out and flung it at Lena. Shocked, Lena bent over and picked up the paper. She opened it up and read the words.

*With Lena*

*Kian.*

"Yeah, Kian followed me out today. Father already told me about the letter, and I told him Kian was fine with me," she said after reading the note.

"Fine?" Eria spat the word. "I was worried to death for him."

"Of course, you were. Sitting in here, working," Lena spat back at her mother.

Eria brought her face close to Lena's and shouted, "You need to be more responsible when it comes to Kian. He's just a little boy; he could have been hurt."

"He's not my responsibility, mother," Lena yelled back. "He's your son, not mine. If anyone needs to be more responsible for him, it's you. You're the one who let him get away without knowing where he went. All you do is sit here working on whatever it is you work on and then chastise both me and Kian for every little thing we do."

Lena's face spun to the side from the slap of her mother's hand. The strike came so fast that Lena didn't see it coming. Tears welled in her eyes immediately. She turned and ran upstairs to her room. Once there, she slammed the door shut and threw herself onto her bed, crying.

This had been an overwhelming day, and she didn't need her mother treating her like this right now. *I hate her sometimes*, she thought. After lying in bed for nearly an hour and collecting her thoughts on the matter, she sat up and remembered that she needed to look up any information she could find on Biotans.

She got to her feet and went to her bookshelf across the room, skimming through the spines of the books she owned. There were several of many different genres, mostly non-fiction, as Lena had taken to reading at a young age. Many things fascinated her, and she loved learning about certain topics as they caught her interest or diving into a new volume brought home by her parents to search for fascinating topics within. One thing that Lena had always been passionate about was outer space, and she knew that she had multiple books on the alien species of the universe.

On Zorath, new prints for paper books, paper books in general, were a bit of a novelty in these times with more advanced alternatives. But, just like her mother, Lena preferred the feeling of a page on her finger and the weight of several in her hand. In fact, she had made it a point for her father to check for the volumes that she was seeking now each time he made it out to the Planetary Bazaar. Once she found the one she was looking for, **'Aliens of the Universe Volume 1 A-F.'** Volumes 1 and 3 were the only two of the series she had paper copies of. They weren't available digitally for some reason, something about the Intergalactic Star Fleet's ruler. She would have her parents looking for volumes 2 and 4 for her each time they made their way off the planet.

"Here we go," she said to herself as she pulled the book off the shelf.

There was a book already sitting on her desk when she sat down. The book was open to a page describing details about the Stinger-class fighter ship, the same ship her father was currently working on in his shop. Researching spacecraft, the vessels of space, was also one of Lena's favorite activities. Whenever her father brought in a new ship to work on, one she had never seen before, she would retrieve her copy of **'Spacecrafts and What Makes Them Work'** and read about the ship. The book was almost completely comprehensive and was the size of an encyclopedia, with plenty of information packed within the pages. Very few times, too few to even mention, would she not be able to find a ship in this book that had passed through her father's shop. Lena did her best to always give her dad some sort of pointer that she would find in the book, even if she had no clue what was wrong with the ship.

Shoving the open book aside, she flipped through to the B's in the book on alien species.

Basili, Beatroixian, Behemah, Bheatalites... There it was—a section for the Biotans. She vaguely remembered skimming across this once but hadn't given these ones much thought. She preferred the weird ones that ate strange things and had strange biological features. If an alien was the size of an island, had an obscene number of legs, or subsisted on plasma, those were the things that stuck in her mind. She hadn't read the B's since she was much younger, and maybe there was some information to give her a better understanding of her new acquaintance. So, she read:

*Biotan: Discovered in 54 ASST by renowned scientist Maximilian Zephyr.Home Planet: Ascendant-2.*

*Domain: N/A Kingdom: N/APhylum: N/A Class: N/A*

*Order: N/A Suborder: N/A Infraorder: N/A*

*Physical Description: Bipedal humanoids that appear almost mechanical.*

*Average weight: N/A - Average height: N/A*

*Skin color: Silvery-gray with a metallic shine.*

*Eye color: White with a black pupil*

*Editor's Note: Much more information has not yet been gathered on the Biotans.*

*Shortly after their discovery, they have gone missing and have not been seen since.*

There was a single photo of a Biotan in the book next to the text. The photo looked similar to Arcturus, but it was apparent that it featured a different Biotan as the subject. This was odd, and it explained why she must have glossed over this one before. Their section was unusually small, and there was almost nothing on them. There was no real detail on the physical description, nothing about their diets or biological functions, and not even an attempt at a cladogram. There was nothing useful here, which was the only thing that was, in fact, very informative.

Lena slammed the book shut, and her eyes went wide. *"I've discovered a lost alien species."* The realization crashed on top of her. *"What could this mean? What the heck does someone do in a situation like this? Should I tell Mother and Father? NO! That's a terrible idea; they wouldn't let me go back."* Her mind raced as she tried to formulate a plan, and she reread the section over and over again, hoping to catch something she might have missed. However, what was on the page was all the information she had to work with. She would have to conduct her own research. A few hours later, she heard her mother shout, "Kian, Lena, dinner."

Lena pulled her nose out of the spacecraft book she was currently reading to take her mind off her predicament, and she made her way downstairs. Kian was holding his handheld gaming device as she came around the corner.

"Kian," Lena said, "Put that back in your room. You know Mother doesn't like it when you bring it to the table."

Kian never looked up and never stopped pushing buttons as he turned and started back upstairs.

"Where's Kian?" Eria said when Lena walked into the dining room.

"Putting his game system up," was all Lena said as she sat down at the table.

"Your father should be in shortly; we'll wait for him before we eat," Eria said to her daughter.

"I know," Lena responded and sat there without saying another word to her mother.

A few moments later, her father walked in holding the power supply pack she had laid on the shelf earlier. Holding it up, he eyed Lena almost sternly. "This thing is fried," Darian said. "I'm not sure what you did with it today, but it won't take charge at all."

Lena started panicking inside. Her brain went into red alert as she began grasping for explanations. She didn't want to tell anyone about Arcturus yet, but she needed to come up with a damn good excuse as to how the power supply pack had overheated and fried.

"We used it to power up Lena's hideout," Kian said as he walked into the room, holding a toy spaceship and flying it through the dining room. "Lena has a cool hideout, and we need it again tomorrow to power it up."

"Well, this one isn't going to work again, Kian," Darian said, tossing it onto the floor by the door. "I'll carry it back to the shop once we're done eating, Eria," he assured his wife.

Kian just saved Lena from having to lie to her parents. True to his word, as always, Kian didn't care if he was lying or if his parents even believed him. He was always telling stories about things that didn't really happen or sometimes about stuff that was almost believable. Lena remained as cool as a cucumber on the outside, or at least she hoped so, but inside, she was wiping her brow with relief.

They all sat quietly and ate for a while, enjoying a meal of slow-roasted avian with steaming sides of bluffbeans and imported sweet corn before Lena spoke up. "Daddy, do you have another power supply pack that I could borrow for tomorrow?"

"No, I'm using the other ones I have to power the fusion thruster on that Stinger. Good suggestion, by the way; that rear thruster was the issue. I knew that was the problem as soon as I started flying it earlier," her father said, a tinge of pride in his voice, though Lena detected a kernel of frustration in there as well. "Not to mention they're too heavy for you to be packing anyway. Luckily, the Star-Trader Bazaar will be in orbit tomorrow or the next day, and I'll be going to resupply. It wouldn't hurt to buy another one while I'm there. That thing was on its last leg as is."

# Chapter 3

## Zorath 6227 ASST

The next day, Lena and Kian returned to the cave after their parents gave permission for him to accompany her. Eria was reluctant to let Kian go but agreed after some convincing from Darian. Arcturus was still there, and he had nearly cleared all the chamber doors of debris. He turned to them when they walked in and asked, "How was your evening?"

It confused Lena how the creature was almost human-like in its actions and the way it spoke. "It was fine," she replied, "other than getting into an argument with my mother."

Arcturus looked up at her seriously. "Did you and her make amends?"

"Not yet. It'll take a couple of days, but we'll be good again before too long," replied Lena dismissively.

"It is very vital to your own health and to the relationship that a human, like you, has with your mother that you two make amends," Arcturus said in his usual robotic and instructional tone, but with something softer than usual mixed in – something like concern.

"I know, we will," she said, irritation in her voice. "Let's change the subject, please." Lena walked over and looked inside the toolbox that was left the day prior. Every tool was there and organized better than her father ever had them. She reached inside and started shuffling them around. "Father would know someone else put these away with them looking like that."

Arcturus tilted his head and watched her for a few moments before he asked, "Why would your father not believe you were the one to put the tools away? I understand he would be correct in his assumption, but how?"

She looked him in the eyes, tilting her head to match his, and said, "Because I've never organized his tools before. Therefore, he would know I wasn't the one who put them away." The way she said this still carried a trace of irritation, even a hint of condescension.

"That is understandable from his perspective. However, why would you not take the time to put the tools away correctly? He did allow you to use them. You allowed me to use them, so I prioritized allocating time toward cleaning and arranging them in an order that would allow your father to contain more tools in the box if he wished."

"I get that," Lena said. "But that's just not how things work. Don't get me wrong; I love and respect my father. He just knows how I am, and I don't want to bring any attention to his mind that you're here. Not yet, at least."

"Once we wake the rest of my people, it will be difficult to hide them from any inhabitants of this world, your parents included," Arcturus informed her.

"I know it." Lena was starting to get anxious about telling Arcturus about the power supply pack. "Speaking of waking the rest of your people, we won't be able to do it today."

"I did assume as much when you did not have the power pack with you," Arcturus replied. He didn't seem very upset at the news. Lena wasn't sure he was even capable of being upset at this rate. "I was correct in my assessment yesterday. It did not have any power."

"Yeah, it was fried," Lena said, very confused. "I thought you just meant it didn't have power left in it."

"No, recharging the power pack was my intended goal when I reached out to it," Arcturus explained. "It would not take any of the power; therefore, my assumption was that it was dead."

Lena looked at him in disbelief. "You're telling me you tried to charge the power supply when, like, lightning was coming out of your fingers?"

Looking back at her with the same disbelief on his face, the most emotion Lena had ever seen the alien express so far, Arcturus replied, "Yes. What else would I have been doing?"

"I guess I thought that little bolt of electricity was just the last bit of energy coming from your awakening. This place was full of electrical energy bolts just moments earlier when your little pod thing opened," Lena said.

Arcturus's gaze now snapped toward Lena, his glowing eyes wide and intently focused on her alone. "Did any of these energy bolts come into contact with you?"

"Umm, yes," Lena said. "Every one of them hit me right in the chest and knocked me across the room. I thought it was going to kill me."

"Oh… My," Arcturus said awkwardly, obviously concerned. It was as if he were trying to formulate an appropriate phrase to express his concern, but he wasn't quite sure if his exclamation made sense to Lena.

It was about that time when they felt a huge rumble in the ground. The cave began to shake, causing tools and cables to rattle and clink wildly around. Kian, who had been perusing the museum of cool robots, fell on his rear.

"Lena!" Kian called for his sister.

"What's happening?" Lena shouted over the noise, fear painted across her face.

"We must go," Arcturus said. "We must leave my people behind for now. They will be safe in their chambers."

Not wanting to stand around and find out if the cave was going to collapse or not, Lena didn't argue. She ran to Kian and scooped him up, then grabbed the toolbox on her way out as they all started towards the entrance. Once they were out of the large room and into the network of corridors, they felt another rumble, this time bone-rattling, and heard the deafening sounds of stones falling and crashing behind them.

"We must hurry, Lena," Arcturus urged. "I may be able to survive these stones falling in on us, but I doubt you or Kian would be able to."

"You'd be correct!" Lena shouted, not slowing her ascent to the cave opening, Kian in her arm, his face buried into her shoulder. They made each turn precisely and moved swiftly. Lena didn't have to think about the way out anymore; she had already been in and out enough times to have this maze memorized. Arcturus followed them both closely behind.

Once they made it to the rope, Lena took hold, handed Kian off to Arcturus, and started climbing. "Once I'm out, I'll need to pull Kian out!" she shouted down as she expediently climbed. "Could you help him get hitched up?"

"Yes," Arcturus replied. He then held Kian in front of him with both outstretched arms, looking the boy in the face. "What does she mean by hitched up?"

"She just wants me to get my foot in this loop so she can pull me out," Kian explained. Clearly scared like Lena, there was also a spark of adventure in the boy's eyes as he looked upon Arcturus. As scared as he was, this was easily the coolest thing that had ever happened to him outside of his video games. "I can do it myself."

Once Kian claimed he could hitch himself up, Arcturus started climbing the rope. He reached the top just as Lena did. "What are you doing?" she asked, her voice cracking with terror and anger all at once. "You were supposed to help Kian."

"He is hitched up," Arcturus explained, then grabbed the rope. "I thought maybe it would be quicker if I were to aid in his ascent."

"Kian!" Lena threw herself on all fours to peer down into the cave, which was quickly filling with a cloud of dust. To her relief, she saw Kian dangling from the end of the rope with his foot placed on the loop, holding on tightly. He looked up at his sister. "I'm ready, Lena!"

"Come on, quickly!" Lena and Arcturus worked together to pull him out, and she found that her new friend was correct. Their teamwork made quick work of getting Kian out; actually, Lena was not quite sure how much she contributed. She might as well have had an industrial mechanism designed for the task, given how effortlessly and smoothly Arcturus brought the rope to the surface.

Though the cave entrance was clear of debris, and she realized there was no immediate danger, Lena still pulled Kian from the entrance as soon as she could reach him and hugged him tightly. "That was so scary," she huffed the words, tears of relief forming under her eyes. "I love you so much, little brother."

"I love you too, Lena." Kian hugged her back, then pulled away to smile at her. She knew it made him happy and always calmed him when she would remind the boy that she loved him. Kian looked up to her more than she believed she deserved to be looked up to by anyone. At least, that was what Lena always believed.

Kian's smile dropped, and he lurched his head around the side of his sister. "Uhh.. Lena," he said, pointing behind her.

She turned, looking in the direction of their home, and saw the heavy black smoke rolling into the sky. Immediately, she got to her feet and started sprinting toward home.

Arcturus followed, keeping pace with Kian so he wouldn't be left behind.

Lena reached her family's property in record time, the edges of her vision fluttering from the exertion of her uninterrupted sprint down and across the rocky terrain. Just as she came into a clear view of it and saw her home, she also saw the destruction. There were three spacecraft hovering over the property. Her father's shop was a crater of billowing black smoke and fire. There was no denying that if anyone were inside the building, they could not still be living. And she knew her father was always in his shop. Lena could only try to keep going, to reach her family and see if they were okay. To see what was happening. But, instead, she fell to her knees mid-sprint, unable to bear what she was witnessing. Her knees slid across the rocky surface, grinding them against pebbles and the sandy ground, but it didn't bother her. The physical pain was entirely absent, drowned out by the deeper, more profound pain that washed over her all at once. She couldn't hold herself up at the thought of her father being dead.

Arcturus approached her from behind, along with Kian. He knelt down beside her and put his arms under her arms, lifting her to a standing position. "We must get you out of the open, Lena. It is not safe here."

"What is going on?" she cried. "Why would someone attack my father?" As she asked the question, she remembered that he once was a member of the Stellarnauts. *Maybe it's someone from his past*, she thought. The thought no more than entered her mind when suddenly, one of the three spacecraft hovering above her property was blown to pieces in a deafening fireball of detonation.

Looking to the sky, she saw a Stinger-class fighter ship barrel through the air. The ship then zipped by, nearly right over them, and as it slowed and performed a flawless 180 maneuver, Lena could see the word 'Starlighter' painted on the side of it in red letters. She almost lost her footing again, realizing it was the same ship her father had been working on for the past few days.

The two remaining ships—Lena was almost positive, from their design, were Spectre-class fighters. They darted after the Stinger that had just destroyed their comrade. They were definitely early models with custom upgrades; being such cheap ships, this made such modifications more cost-efficient. Lena noticed that they had equipped themselves with laser cannons mounted on retractable hardpoints located on the bottom of their chassis.

Spectres typically didn't come equipped with such firepower; however, the Stinger did. Neither one of the ships was equipped with pulse shields, making both easy targets in a dogfight. That very weapon told Lena that the Spectres were possibly being piloted by space pirates looking to score some loot from this planet, possibly even to upgrade more of their ships. *"But why would they destroy the shop?"* Lena wondered. *"Some of the most valuable equipment in this world was in there. Were they that stupidly ruthless, or was this some kind of revenge against my daddy after all?"*

The two Spectres took off after the solo Stinger, firing their laser cannons at the fleeing ship. The Stinger was quick and agile, and, from the looks of it, so was the pilot, allowing them to evade the incoming blasts with ease. They flew out of view in hot pursuit. Lena decided now was the best opportunity to make her way all the way down to the property where the once-renowned Zoravic's shop sat in ruin.

Arcturus and Kian followed her, each of them trying to be as quiet as possible yet moving as fast as they could. As they got closer, they observed a man on the ground near the seemingly intact house. He was wearing some sort of dark uniform with a long black coat that ran to his knees. This man had someone on the ground outside the front door of her home, holding a gun to her head. The person on the ground was Eria, her mother, who appeared beaten, bloody, and sobbing.

*"What were these people looking for that would cause them to do this to my family?"*

48

Her mind screamed for answers. Lena knew her father kept a blaster in his shop, but with the amount of damage to the building, it would be too dangerous to go inside to seek it out.

The three made their way closer to the house. Lena wanted to see if they could hear what the intruders were saying. So, they approached carefully, doing their best to keep the larger stones and sparse brush between them and anyone who may spot them.

"What's happened-" Kian started before one of Arcturus's hands made a seal around the child's mouth, and Kian found himself in the extraterrestrial's arms again.

They listened closely. No one was saying anything, but Lena could hear a faint static in the air. She tried to concentrate on the sound. Without warning, an explosion came from the distance behind them. Then, the static sound was gone, and a crackling, feminine voice was heard. "Captain, Ace is down. We're going to need help with this one. This guy's the real deal."

Lena peeked around the bend of the stone she was hiding behind. The tall, lean man with slicked-back hair, piercing blue eyes, and a smirk on his face turned that smirk to the sky, lifted his forearm beside his face, and spoke into it with a sneer. "Mouse, send two more ships down here to help your Sergeant. She can't handle a solo Stinger on her own."

"Aye, Captain." Another female voice came over the device on his wrist. "Streak and Rocket are en route now, Captain." Within a few moments, two more Spectres dove out of the clouds and leveled out, heading for the location of their companion. The man seemingly in charge turned his attention back to Lena's mother. His clothing appeared more like some hand-tailored outfit than a pirate's typical attire. It was unusually formal, with a black vest, an off-white collared shirt, and even a string tie. Each piece was made of a clothy material, unlike the common polymers of every other outfit Lena had ever seen on a real person. His dark jacket appeared almost like cracking leather toward the bottom, reaching down to the knees of his pants. Below them, the ends of his pant legs and dress shoes appeared dirty and worn, in stark opposition to the rest of the well-kept visage above them.

"We need to get down there and free my mother," Lena said, looking at Arcturus.

"I am no combatant, Lena," Arcturus said. "And my power source is very limited at this moment due to the amount used in the awakening of technomancy in you."

Lena's eyes never left Arcturus when she asked, "What?"

"We should possibly discuss this at a later time," Arcturus replied. "Getting you to safety is currently of the utmost importance."

Another explosion came from the distance, and the strangely dressed man lifted his forearm again and asked, "Is the Stinger down?"

"Not yet, Captain," the same female voice came back. "He took out Streak as soon as he engaged with the Stinger. I don't know who this pilot is, but we may have to recruit him rather than fight him."

"To hell with that," the captain yelled. "He's already blown up three of my ships. I want him dead."

Lena looked at Arcturus and whispered, "Three ships? What about the three pilots he's killed?"

Arcturus just shrugged and said, "Let us move away from this location; it is not safe here. Kian, stay close to Lena and myself."

"Arcturus, we have to save my mother," Lena protested with tears in her eyes, knowing she hadn't had the chance to make up with her mother after the fight they had the night before.

"Lena, if we go down there right now, we risk losing more than just your mother," Arcturus said. "Logically, it makes the most sense for us to hide and wait for either your father, who I assume is piloting the Stinger-class ship the captain is speaking of, to destroy the remaining enemy ships and then come to defeat the captain. Or we wait until the dogfight is over and the enemies leave the planet once they get what they have come for."

"Logically?" Lena spat. "We can't just hide while these people destroy my whole family."

She turned and started making her way closer to where her mother was being held. The captain was holding an old-world handgun to her mother's head—a revolver, a six-shooter, they were called if memory served her correctly. He had a leather holster at his side, apparently made special to fit such a weapon.

"Who's flying that Stinger?" the captain asked her mother through clenched teeth, the gun pushed hard against her head. "That pilot is destroying all my ships."

Eria looked the captain right in the eyes and said, "My husband is piloting that ship, and you better start counting your moments because once he's finished taking out your crew, he'll be coming back here for you, too." Another explosion came just as her mother finished saying those words, almost as a promise that this was going to happen.

"Captain," the woman's voice came over the radio again.

"Aye," the captain said. "Rodriguez, you better be radioing in to let me know that the last explosion was that Stinger. Apparently, he wasn't in the shop. Bastard."

"Aye, Captain," Rodriguez replied. "Rocket and I were able to corner him and take him out. He and Rocket were both shot down simultaneously. I'm on my way back now."

"Daddy, no," Lena whispered.

"Looks like your husband ain't the pilot you thought him to be, madam," the captain said to Eria, the smirk returning. "Now that bit of fun is out of the way, I have a few questions for you."

Eria slumped forward, tears rolling down her cheeks. She shook her head back and forth, saying through sobs and tears, "You're wrong. Darian isn't dead; he can't be. He was the best pilot; he couldn't be defeated by scum like yourselves."

"Scum?" the captain yelled. "The name Captain Jaxson Blackwood is as renowned as it is feared, and you think I'm scum? I'll show you scum." He turned his revolver back on Eria and pulled the trigger. The sound echoed through the hills behind Lena as she jumped back from the loud explosion the small weapon made. The blast from the revolver was much more than Lena would have ever thought possible. The sound reverberated through her gut, but not nearly as much as the sight of the shot's consequences. Her mother, Eria, fell forward, her face smacking the ground limply. She lay there, unmoving.

Lena was waiting to wake from this nightmare, but the milliseconds dragged on, and she never did. She was awake. Her mother and father had been ripped from her by a madman, and

52

he was going to pay. He had to. Without thinking, she started toward him.

Arcturus extended an arm to catch Lena as soon as he noticed what she was doing. He managed to halt her with a grip on her shoulder, but in his reactive state, desperate to keep Lena safe, Kian wriggled himself out of Arcturus's other hand. The awkward leverage he had on the boy due to his lunge and the extension of his arm allowed Kian to escape. As soon as his little feet hit the ground, he was already scrambling through the brush. "Momm…" Kian started as he dashed away from Arcturus and began running towards his mother. As soon as the boy appeared in clear view, Captain Blackwood instinctively turned and fired his weapon once more. The small boy didn't get to finish his last word before a bullet from the weapon struck him in the chest, and he, too, fell over, lying no more than thirty feet from his mother.

Lena screamed out after trying to hold her emotions in. Hearing that her father was shot down and seeing her mother gunned down was enough, but she couldn't hold back any longer upon seeing Kian lying on the red dirt before her, lifeless.

Arcturus's grip loosened upon hearing the gunshot, just long enough for Lena to continue her path. She reached out for Kian, moving in his direction. Captain Blackwood turned his attention to her, and she to him. At that moment, Mouse's voice came back over his wrist device, "Captain, a Stellarnaut ship just entered Zorath's orbit. I think it's time we come back home so we can get out of here."

"Mouse, I need that power source," the captain said. "Our targets have been eliminated, but that energy surge we picked up is here. I can feel it."

"Captain Blackwood," Mouse's voice was stern and demanding. "I understand you're the captain of this ship, but I think it's very relevant that I make myself clear. A Stellarnaut transport ship just entered orbit. If you don't return to the ship in the next five minutes, you and Sergeant Rodriguez will be Stellarnaut prisoners, and Mouse will be the captain of this fine new **Scorpion** we just obtained on our last venture."

Lena's thoughts turned to hatred. Without knowing why, she stretched her arm out as if she were going to pierce a hole through Blackwood's chest. Her other arm reached back; she could feel something coming from Arcturus. Her body was filled with energy, not unlike the energy she felt when she had first woken up Arcturus. It was similar to the way she was blasted across the chamber, but only this time, it felt as though she was taking the energy inside herself. The energy flowed from Arcturus and then through Lena. She could feel the energy pulsating throughout her entire body as if it would cause her to explode from the inside. The pressure built so fast that Lena screamed out in pain before the pressure was gone. She felt the energy leave her body through the fingertips of the hand she had stretched towards Blackwood. The blast struck him right in the chest and face. He lost his grip on his revolver and was knocked back.

Lena collapsed, her body weakened from what had just happened to it. Exhausted and confused a few moments later, she rolled onto her back and glanced to see Arcturus kneeling on the ground. His chest was glowing bright white, but it was fading.

"Are you okay?" she asked, not knowing why, only the thought that whatever had just happened was a direct cause of him.

"I will be fine," Arcturus responded as he began to rise to his feet. He walked over and helped Lena stand. The two of them made their way over to where Blackwood lay on the ground. They stopped when he began to move. She couldn't believe it; she saw a huge blast of energy strike the man dead in the center of his chest. *"How is he still alive?"* She asked herself, *"For that matter, how am I still alive when it happened to me? Why am I, now?"*

Blackwood rolled over and pushed himself to his feet. Smoke still rolled from his chest and the top of his head. He held his hands over his face. When he lowered them to look towards Lena and Arcturus, Lena could see that his face was burnt. Black lines resembling lightning bolts ran up his face from his chest.

He raised his wrist to his mouth and, with a raspy voice, said, "Rodriguez, come get me."

The Spectre flew in and hovered just over the captain. A ladder lowered from the underbelly. Blackwood reached up and grabbed the ladder; he winced in pain but persevered. The ship lifted, and he ascended with it, climbing into the cockpit as the ladder retracted within. They disappeared into the clouds from which they had come.

As the attackers lifted away, Lena ran over and scooped her little brother's body up into her arms. She sat there and held him as his lifeless eyes stared back at her. She gently brushed his eyelids shut and held him close. Lost in her emotions, she stayed in that moment quietly, without the energy to even sob. As tears poured slowly from her eyes, she never noticed how the time passed or the people who had been walking toward her. Arcturus, who had watched on silently before the others arrived, now stood over Lena as she mourned the loss of her family, facing the newcomers. He wasn't going to let anyone come near her.

# Chapter 4

## Zorath

### 6227 ASST

Lena didn't know how long she had kneeled there, in that spot. The spot where her life had been ripped away from her. She was still holding Kian in her arms when she heard a man clear his throat a few paces from her."Excuse me, miss. I am Captain Janus Zephyr of the Stellarnaut Armada. We were near this planet when we received a distress call from one of my old comrades, Darian Zoravic. The call came from this location on the planet. Do you know where I could find him?

Just the mention of her father's name caused Lena to start crying all over again. It took some time before she could compose herself enough to answer the man, the captain. He stood firm and patient while she sat there and cried into the shoulder of her little brother's lifeless body. Finally, she looked up to address the man who spoke to her. He was younger than Lena had expected, judging by the sound of his voice and his rank as a captain. He stood there, hands behind his back, head held high, and a look of remorse on his face. His hair was dark and longer than she would have thought for a soldier, and his eyes were bluer than the clearest sky she'd ever seen. The suit he wore was not much different from the one her father wore in the photograph sitting on the shelf in their home. The suit ~~he wore~~ was predominantly black, with silver accents, one of which stood out on the upper left chest plate. It read the word

'*Zephy*'; Lena wasn't sure if it was his name etched there or not because the other soldiers around her each had the same word etched on the same spot of their suits as well. There was a white glow coming from within the suit that traced along the natural seams and joints of the body. A helmet hung at Janus's hip, and it, too, was of the same color and had the same white through the seams.

Her father's suit was gray in color, similar to the other Stellarnaut soldiers who were with Captain Zephyr. She recalled there being lettering on the chest plate as well, but they were too small in the photo for her to make out. This must be a newer Stellarnaut suit design than the one her father wore before he left the Armada. "Darian Zoravic was my father," Lena choked out a response. You're too late to speak to him. The other space crew that was here killed him along with..." Lena looked over to her mother and back down to Kian. Tears welled again, and she continued, "My mom and Kian."

"You're little Lena..." Captain Zephyr spoke with a hushed realization and reached down to help Lena to her feet. "I am sorry for your--"

"Do not touch her," Arcturus demanded, stepping in between Lena and Janus. "I will assist her if she feels she needs it. For now, she must mourn the loss of her little human brother, Kian, and her parents, whom I was unable to meet before their demise."

It's fine, Arcturus," Lena said, lowering Kian to the ground and standing on her own feet. "How long ago did my father send his distress call? I'm sure he would have thought you could have made it before they died," Lena never looked up from Kian's body as she spoke.

"It was twenty-three minutes before we flew into the orbit of Zorath," Captain Zephyr replied.

"We tend to answer distress calls as soon as possible, especially those from former Stellarnauts. We were quite close to your planet when the transmission was received, Miss Zoravic," another one of the Stellarnaut soldiers said as he stepped closer. He, too, was a very young-looking man. His skin tone was slightly darker than Captain Zephyr's, with close-cropped black hair, not unlike her father's in the photo. His eyes were dark brown and almond-shaped, with a double eyelid unlike any she'd ever seen. "Would you mind if I take a look at your vital signs?" he asked. "We would like to make sure you didn't sustain any injuries before we arrived on the planet."

"Dr. Kim," Zephyr stepped in. "Give the young lady a moment. She doesn't seem to show any signs of injury." Dr. Kim turned his attention to Arcturus.

"These junior doctors always want to make sure their position is warranted, and Dr. Kim here is a recent graduate of the academy," Captain Zephyr added, nodding toward the young doctor.

"Arcturus," Dr. Kim said once he'd turned his attention to Lena's robotic friend, fascination evident on his face as he spoke the Biotan's name almost as if it were a question. "Would you mind if I looked at your vitals? I would like to make sure you didn't sustain any injuries, either."

"You may inspect me if it will divert your attention away from Lena for a moment," Arcturus granted. "Although, I assure you, you will find no damage to my body."

Dr. Kim's suit was the same shape and design as Captain Zephyr's, with the exception that his suit was predominantly white with blue accents. The same white glow ran along the seams and joints, though they were harder to make out against the white of his suit. Every other soldier—there were four other soldiers in this landing party, other than Captain Zephyr and Dr. Kim—was wearing a gray suit. Each of their suits was of the same design: black accents and white glowing lines. They were masked behind the full-face visor of their helmets and were spread out, assessing the damages around the property.

"What is going to happen now?" Lena asked the captain.

"Now we assess the damages, try to figure out what happened here, and then try to track down and bring the perpetrators to justice," Janus Zephyr answered concisely.

"What happened? That's easy," Lena said. "A pirating crew, or whatever they were, led by a tyrant; a tyrant who called himself Captain Blackwood came here, blew up my dad's shop, killed my family, and didn't even take anything. I'm not the smartest person, but I believe this was more than just a robbery gone wrong."

"Thank you for your assessment. I have heard of Blackwood. He's a notorious pirate known for scavenging and some minor crimes, but nothing of this magnitude," Captain Zephyr said. "But we will still do a thorough investigation of the property and assess the damages."

"How long will you all be here? And how long will the investigation take?" Lena asked.

"In most cases, similar to this," He paused for a moment, tilting his head slightly as though deep in thought. "I would think we should be finished up here and leaving this planet by morning."

"Good," Lena said. "That gives me time to take care of my family and gather my belongings before we leave."

Janus looked down at her. The ~~look~~ expression on his face told her ~~that~~ he did not agree with her assessment of the situation. "Before we," he emphasized, "—leave? You are not accompanying us when we depart this planet, Miss Zoravic?"

"I most certainly am," she replied firmly. "My father, a Stellarnaut veteran, called you here to defend his family. I do not feel defended or protected, so until the pirate crew who killed my family are captured and dealt with, it is your duty as part of the Stellarnaut Armada to protect me. My father may not have spoken much about his time in the Stellarnauts, but he taught me some of the by-laws of how the Stellarnauts operate. I remember that quite clearly."

"The best protection for you would be to stay here with a social worker. You have no idea what's out there, Lena."

"I will never feel protected from them until I know for a fact that they have paid for this," Lena protested.

"And so, I'll notify you when that hap…"

"I need to see it! I need to know," Lena interrupted the captain. "They took my family! You say you knew my daddy. I assume you were friends, so they took him from both of us." Her voice cracked with emotion.

Captain Zephyr closed his eyes and pinched his brow just above the bridge of his nose. "Very well," he sighed and looked back at Lena sternly. "I'm sure your father knew what he was doing when he summoned us. I would assume he meant for us to be taking the rest of his family, as well, if I remember anything about Darian at all. I am sorry that he had to go like this. I would have loved to have him back in my company. I wanted to see him again. Hopefully, he doesn't haunt me if anything happens to you. Your Dad was a dangerous man."

"How did you know my dad, anyway?" Lena asked. "You can't be much older than me, and he left the Armada years before I was born."

The captain chuckled a bit. "Darian Zoravic never told you who his captain was?"

"No, like I said, he never really talked much about his time in the Stellarnauts," Lena replied.

"Yes, it would seem not. I am the captain of the Ascendant 4, the Atlas-class ship my father, Maximilian Zephyr, had built the day I was born so I could captain it when I came of age. I was captain of that same ship the entire time your father served under me on it. And I have captained that very ship for nearly nine hundred years."

"Nine hundred years?" she questioned. "If that is true, and if my father served you, you must be an excellent captain" Lena said, just as something caught her attention. She walked over to where Captain Blackwood had dropped the gun he used to kill her mother and brother. She bent over, picked it up, and examined the weapon. The barrel was blue steel with a design that looked like smoke engraved down its length. The cylinder was smoked steel with the word "Col" etched into it, and the handle was pearl white with the word "Peacemaker" engraved on it, starting from the bottom and working its way up and around the curve. *This couldn't have been Blackwood's decision,* she thought after seeing the word.

Captain Zephyr stepped beside her and looked down past her shoulder at the gun she held. "Not always. But your father… he was an excellent Stellarnaut, a great friend, and the best damn pilot I've ever known" Captain Zephyr then rested a hand on her shoulder. Even with the suit's advanced, hard exterior, the gesture felt gentle and reassuring. "I miss him, too."

After a brief examination of the firearm, Lena opened the revolving chamber. *"Four more."* She snapped it back into place with a flick of her wrist and tucked it into her waistband. She then walked over to where Dr. Kim had some sort of a medical device that Lena had never seen before hooked to Arcturus's arms.

"Your vitals are unlike anything I have ever seen before," Dr. Kim said as she walked up.

"Of course they are," Arcturus said. "I am certain you have never met another being like myself anywhere in the galaxy."

"Arcturus," Lena said as she walked up to where he and the doctor were.–"Will you help me gather my things and maybe…" She cleared her throat, inhaling deeply through her nose, trying to maintain her strong exterior in the presence of these great heroes she had always dreamed about meeting under better circumstances. She was hesitant to say the next part as if it would make the truth more real than it currently was. "Could you maybe help me bury my family?"

Arcturus pulled the cuffs off his arms and stepped away from Dr. Kim. "Of course, Lena. I also overheard you telling the captain that we would accompany them once they leave this planet. Is that correct?"

"Yes," Lena replied. "With my family gone.." Lena winced a little, saying the words: *"Family gone"* out loud. It pained her how matter-of-fact she felt ~~that~~ she needed to be about the ordeal. The wounds were still so fresh, and she knew they would be for a long time. But she fought back more tears, the urge to remember, and cleared her throat as she continued, "There's nothing left for me here, and this is the only way I'll be able to see to it that the people who did this are dealt with accordingly."

"The only way *we* will be able to see to it," Arcturus corrected her as he stepped in closer, right before her. He made the same strange gesture with his right hand that he did back in the cave when he vowed to protect her father's tools. "You have my word as a Biotan and as an independent entity that I will stand by your side and see to it that you see justice brought to the people who have wronged you and your family."

Lena stared at her strange new friend. The gesture was not so alien to her as it was the first time. She knew then that she still had someone left, at least. Someone who could keep her close to home. "Thank you, Arcturus. I know you mean that."

Arcturus's hand returned to normal, and then the two walked to the rubble that was once her father's shop. "We need to find some wood to build a coffin. We can bury my mother and Kian together. Hopefully, we can retrieve Father. I would love to be able to lay him to rest if we can find him as well or any of the pilots at all, really. Aerial laser cannons don't typically leave remains."

Captain Zephyr approached Lena and Arcturus. "If I may interrupt Lena, I think we can handle making the preparations for your family's final resting place. I hope to lay Darian with Eria and your brother, but your assessment is correct. If the ship that shot him down was equipped with a laser cannon, it would make recovery difficult. My crew and I would have an easier time locating the wreckage, anyway. If he's there, we'll get him." He was clearly trying to be polite so as not to overstep Lena's boundaries. "This will give you more time to gather the belongings you'll need. Take your time; leaving your home behind isn't easy."

"Thank you, that would be very helpful," Lena spoke with a tone of appreciation as she looked up at the significantly taller man.

"Arcturus and I will get the things we need. We'll meet you later for the ceremony." Janus nodded and turned to approach his ship but stopped when he felt a small hand take hold of his wrist to halt him. He turned back. "Again… thank you," Lena told him. She saw the gleam of compassion in the captain's eyes as he nodded once more and continued on his way. As she watched him walk away to begin his search for her father's body, reality came crashing over her again, and her tough facade fell. She put her face into her hands, lowered to her knees, and she bawled.

Arcturus rested his pale hand on her back, just below her neck, and rubbed it gently up and down. "Losing loved ones is very difficult. The pain will ease with time, but you will never forget. Their memories live on through you." His heartfelt words were juxtaposed by his robotic cadence, but they warmed Lena all the same.

Lena reached up and put her hand over his. His skin felt oddly similar to hers, with the exception of being cold to the touch. She sniffled through her labored breathing as her sobbing subsided. "Your hand… it feels so much more like mine than I would have thought possible."

"I can alter my externality to fit the situation," he informed her, his voice as stoic as ever. "In fact, if the situation arises for defense or combat, like earlier, for instance, I can make my outer layer as hard as..." He tilted his head as though he were thinking again. "Steel?" He questioned himself. "Is steel the correct term?" He asked Lena.

"Yes," she smiled, and a suppressed snort left her nose. Even with the heartache, it was nice to smile and laugh. Lena was glad she'd found Arcturus and that he was now a part of her life. "Steel would be a good term for something very hard. Come on, let's go inside the house and get some stuff that we'll need for the trip."

Lena took Arcturus by his wrist, and he pulled her to her feet before the two walked over to her home and went through the front door. Around them, the Stellarnaut landing party worked to investigate the property, trying to gather any information they could as to why the pirate crew had landed there. To answer the question: *What was it that made the Zoravic family home their target?*

While walking through the main family room, Lena's instinctual glance went to the picture of her father, the one she had stopped and admired many times in the past. There, like he always was, in his Stellarnaut uniform: gray armor, black accents, and the white glow from within, just like Captain Zephyr's. The only difference is his suit seemed to be of an older design. The armor of her father's suit appeared more built-in and bulkier than what the Stellarnauts outside were wearing, leading Lena to conclude that they must have updated the design since he left the force. She picked up the picture and held it against her chest for a moment before pulling it back and looking into his eyes once more.

She looked at Arcturus. "Do you eat?" she asked him.

"It is not a requirement," Arcturus replied. "Biotans can eat to analyze the properties of various materials; however, the digestive process is rather unenjoyable."

"Gross," Lena said, feeling sorry that she asked. "I just wanted to see if you could go into the kitchen and gather some food. Preferably some that won't spoil soon."

"Certainly. If you could point me in the direction of the kitchen, I would gladly gather some provisions for our journey."

Lena pointed him in the right direction, instructing him not to get anything from the refrigerator. Once Arcturus was on his way, she turned and went upstairs. In her bedroom, lying on the bed, was a folded piece of parchment. It was propped up against the pillow on a bed she knew she hadn't taken the time to make that morning. Feeling the tears starting to well in her eyes again, she sat on the edge of the bed and picked up the parchment.

Holding the paper in her hands, she slowly started unfolding it. Once open, it read;

Lena,

I'm sorry for the way I acted the other night. I know how much Kian loves being with you, and I'm sure you had nothing to do with him following you. Please forgive me, and if you would like, I'd like for you and me to spend the day together tomorrow. I could use a break from work anyway. Come see me when you're ready.

Love Mom!

After reading those final words from her mother, she folded the paper back up. She buried her face in her loose blanket and cried once more. She thought of the last thing she'd said to her mother, her final thoughts about her. If only she'd known. If only she would have cared to realize that this could happen. She wondered if she was a bad daughter. She wondered what her mother's final thoughts were and if they were similar to the ones that she was having now. She imagined the fear and pain that she must have gone through and wondered why that had to be their departing words. None of it was fair.

After a few minutes of processing everything, Lena remembered Arcturus and that she needed to gather her belongings. She got back to her feet, tucked the photo of her father into the fold of the note from her mother, set both on her desk and began rummaging through her things. She decided that a couple of changes of clothing and her books on spacecraft and alien species were what she was going to bring. The note and photo about spacecraft went in the center of the spacecraft book, in the chapter covering the Stinger, stored away nice and safe. It was all that went into her backpack besides the stuff she normally took on her adventures away from home. Then she said goodbye to her room.

Kian's bedroom was right down the hall, so she stepped inside. She sat on his bed for a moment, rubbing her hand against his blanket a few times as she looked around the room. She'd always loved the soft material her mother used to make blankets for Kian - handmade, just like her childhood blankets and cold-season clothes. She would always donate them to the nearby village when the kids outgrew her creations. Handmade clothes, paper books, and neighborly consideration: Eria was old-school in her sensibilities and preferences to the end.

Lena stood back up and walked over to Kian's little desk, picking up the handheld gaming system he would play in the evening while they waited for dinner. This is what she would take of his, to remember him by. Maybe even playing the games, he would always tell her she should try, but she had never been interested in it until now. She stuffed it, along with its charging cable, into her bag and left the room. Just before she shut the door, she turned and took one last look into the room of the little brother she would never see again.

Lena went back downstairs, walked into the dining room, and sat in her chair at the table. She looked around the room, remembering the times she had sitting there talking to her family, enjoying their company. She closed her eyes and imagined her family sitting there with her. Her Dad laughed at something that Kian was doing. He would look up and smile at her, a gesture he did that she always loved. Her mom brought the final tray, sitting it down on the table before removing her apron and sitting down to join them. She would never have that again.

Inhaling through her nose, she took in the scent of home. She could smell the last meal her mom cooked, the soap her father would use to wash his hands before dining. The smell of home would be gone forever, too. Reluctantly, Lena got to her feet and said, "Arcturus, are you ready?" The odd being walked from the kitchen, and she got up, and they left the house.

When she stepped outside, it was getting dark, and the Stellarnauts had already arranged a nice burial site for her mother and Kian not too far from the front of the house. They both lay in a single wooden box. Eria lay with her right arm tucked up under Kian as though they were lying down for a nap, and he was cuddling her. Her other arm was folded up on her chest, and both of their eyes were closed. The young doctor had done an excellent job of covering up the wound on her head. Lena hadn't even noticed it. She couldn't help but smile at the way they looked just before she lost it once more and fell to her knees. Arcturus was there to catch and comfort her in her time of need.

"I'm sorry, Lena," Janus said. She hadn't noticed him approach. "We found the wreckage of a Stinger but no sign of Darian. None of you deserved this. A man like him…" He paused, at a loss for words. He seemed unsure of what he could say or if he should say anything at all. "If there is anything you need, anything at all…" He turned to the rest of the ground party, who had now removed their helmets and stood solemnly around the scene of grieving. "We're here for you."

"Could I have a moment alone with them before they are put in the ground?" She asked no one in particular but everybody as one. Each Stellarnaut who was there, Captain Zephyr included, relayed their understanding and walked away. Arcturus stayed for a moment, but Lena only needed to look at him, and he, too, understood and turned to walk away from the hastily built wooden casket.

Lena reached down inside and took her mother by the hand. "I'm sorry too, Mommy," she cried. "I wish I would have been a better daughter to you. I'm so sorry for all the trouble I caused you and all the fights we had. I wish I could take it back… I love you so much." Her voice cracked as she forced herself through her departing words, the ones she hoped her mother could hear now. "I hope you know that."

# Chapter 5

## Zorath

## 6227 ASST

After a restless night, Lena rose early and went to the grave of her family. She ran her hand along the piece of wood she had placed there for the grave marker the night before. It read:

*In Loving Memory of the Zoravic Family*

*You will be missed.*

Lena turned to Arcturus, who had awaited her all night and joined her as she left the resting quarter of the Stellarnaut's landing ship. She had insisted on sleeping there last night. Staying in the husk of her old home would have been too painful. She had already bid farewell to the place, anyway. "I'm ready to go." She wasn't; she wished she could stay with them a while longer, but she'd already held the landing party up long enough as it was.

Arcturus led Lena back towards where the Stellarnauts had landed their ship. It was a Phoenix starship, the same kind her dad had flown when he was a Stellarnaut pilot. Much larger than the Stinger, it was capable of carrying up to ten passengers. The Stinger is meant for a single pilot and perhaps one co-pilot, though the latter is not required to fly. The Phoenix ship is designed for long-range exploration and military operations. Its hull is composed of advanced alloys reinforced with pulse shields, providing excellent protection against enemy fire. With its sleek, aerodynamic design and bird-like shape, it possesses a striking appearance. It seems to have the same white glow coming from within as the Stellarnaut's suits do.

Maximilian Zephyr was aboard the **Phoenix Ascendant**, a ship designed by him, Laura Sivik, and Kraytus Sivik, the now self-proclaimed emperor of the galaxy. It was the same ship that the first humans, including the designers themselves, had left Earth on when stellar space travel first became possible for them. The galaxy wouldn't be what it is today had it not been for the three of them so many years ago.

Maximilian named the Stellarnauts' main transport ships and fighter ships after the first spaceship he helped create. Lena was certain that she would no doubt be boarding an Atlas-class transport ship once they reached Zorath's orbit. Zephyr named each of his Atlas ships "Ascendant," followed by the number indicating the order in which they were built, except for the first ten numbers. Maximilian Zephyr reserved those for the ten children he planned on having. However, he only had four children, and Lena didn't know how old Captain Zephyr was, but the number on his ship should place him as the first through fourth born of all Maximilian Zephyr's children.

A ramp lowered down from under the hull of the Phoenix, pressing itself into the reddish soil and allowing her, Arcturus, and the Stellarnaut crew, who were outside, to board the ship.

Once the ramp retracted behind them and the hatch closed, Lena found herself back in the Phoenix's cabin. This time, the surrounding crew had their backs against the walls of the cabin, inside sections designed for them to fit in place, where they could stand, sit, or even lean back in a resting position. It was in one of these unoccupied spaces where she had tried so fruitlessly to rest the night before.

Captain Zephyr's voice resonated through the intercom, reaching the passengers' ears. "Ready for takeoff." The words flowed out in a way that made it clear he had uttered them countless times before and was simply going through the motions of procedure. Lena took her place in the same spot as the night before, right beside Arcturus. The Biotan had just enough time to strap the two into place before the captain had fired the engines, hit the thrusters, and lifted off.

The sudden takeoff and proceeding motion sent a fluttering sensation deep through Lena's abdomen. She looked around and noticed that the rest of the crew weren't even strapped into place, as if the backs of their suits were magnetized to the wall behind them, and none of them seemed the least bit bothered by the takeoff. One of them even read a holo-script.

This was going to be the first time Lena had ever gone off-world. She had never even gone to the market with her Dad during the times the Star Trader Bazaar had come to orbit above Zorath. Her knees trembled almost as much at the travel itself as at the thought of leaving her home and her family behind. These weren't the circumstances she wanted to be in when she finally left Zorath, but she had always wanted to join the Stellarnauts and travel the galaxy like her dad did. So, at least she was, kind of, doing that. It hardly made her feel any better about it, though.

She was strapped in, but the bridge at the front of the Phoenix had a curved viewpoint and a three-hundred-and-sixty-degree vertical view, allowing her to watch the planet expand as Phoenix ascended. Zorath was beautiful from this point of view.

She had never realized just how many shades of red defined the visuals of her home planet. The soil appeared almost like brush strokes, making her already miss the place even more. The leaves of the forests were dominated by various reddish hues. This was something Lena had never seen much of before, not much beyond some spots up high at the edges of the mesa, where she could catch a glimpse of the tops of the forest edge way off in the distance. Lena had never ventured much more than a few miles from her home, as much as she loved exploring. In just a few swift moments, she had already seen more of Zorath's surface than she had in her sixteen years of living here. It was beautiful.

Before she knew it, her attention was turned upwards as they left the planet's atmosphere at an uninterrupted speed that baffled Lena as to how she couldn't feel the force of it much stronger than she was. Just ahead of them, suspended in the void of Zorath's exosphere, was the most beautiful spacecraft Lena had ever seen. It was a Stellarnaut Capital ship with the words "Ascendant 4" written on the side of it. The letters were taller than her father's workshop, which was long. The Atlas, as she knew, were streamlined Stellarnaut transport ships that appeared like massive shuttlecraft. They had sleek hulls with flattened bottoms, allowing them to land on and take off from planetary surfaces, though they hardly ever entered a planet's atmosphere. Standing before one now, Lena saw firsthand the large cargo bay at the ship's rear and the spacious cockpit located at the forward end. She knew from her studies that troop transport would be found in the ship's center, with the closed hangar hatches on its sides further compounding this.

A cargo bay hatch opened up on the side of the Atlas, near the rear of the ship, as they approached. Spinning lights of a bright, white hue activated, and a spray of gaseous substance, likely oxygen, emanated from outlets along the door's vertices as the hangar opened. Lena imagined the hiss of the gas and the sounds of the heavy mechanisms one would expect from such a sight, if not for the silencing void of space, as the Phoenix gracefully entered the transport corridor that swiftly led them to another hangar door while the first closed behind them. Smoothly, this door opened and allowed the crew entry into the largest interior space Lena had ever been in. There were nearly fifty more Phoenix spacecraft parked throughout the bay, along with multiple Stellarnaut troops milling around doing duties.

When they landed, there were several troops wearing suits similar to the gray ones worn by the Stellarnauts around her. There were many more wearing what appeared to be simple jumpsuits, not much different from what her father wore while working in his shop. Lena got to her feet, Arcturus at her side. The ramp lowered down, and the captain, along with the other members of the crew, descended from the Phoenix. Lena and Arcturus followed. With only the bag slung over her shoulder, Lena didn't allow any of them to assist her with it. No matter how much they tried, this bag contained everything she had left from her family.

"Lena," Captain Zephyr addressed the young lady as she examined the landing bay, "I must be off; there is much to do. A captain's work never ceases. I'm going to turn you over to one of my trusted specialists. Patel, you're with them." He pointed at Lena and Arcturus.

"Hello," one soldier said as he walked up to her and Arcturus. He held a holo-script and looked up at Arcturus with momentary surprise before politely adjusting his expression and offering a handshake. "I'm Ryan Patel. I'm a junior technician. In other words, I just do what I'm instructed by my superiors."

"Hello, Ryan Patel; my name is Arcturus," Arcturus said. "This is my friend Lena… Lena." He turned toward Lena, slight confusion on his face, and asked, "Zoravic?"

"Yes, Arcturus," Lena said. She reached out her hand and said, "Nice to meet you, Ryan, I'm Lena…Lena Zoravic." She gave Arcturus a wry smile. The gesture seemed lost on him.

Ryan took her hand and shook it, his eyes squinting and his head turned up as though he was thinking about something. He said the name over and over to himself but loud enough to be heard. "Zoravic… Zoravic…" He trailed off. "That name sounds familiar." Ryan offered his hand to Arcturus, who stared at it. Ryan pulled back his and said, "Well, um, here, follow me. I'm to show you where you'll be sleeping for the duration of the trip."

"I do not sleep," Arcturus said, following closely behind Lena and Ryan.

They left the holding bay, going up a flight of stairs that led to a long hallway with doors on each side. "This is the barracks," Ryan said as they walked down the hall at the top of the stairs. "Most of the troops on this ship stay in this area. This is the central hall. There are two more just like this on each side of the ship. We house over one thousand troops on this one vessel."

"You know, I've always wanted to see a Stellarnaut barracks hall," Lena said, looking around. "Really wanted it to be after I graduated from the academy, though. I can't believe there are so many rooms in one ship. It's like a floating city up here."

Lena smiled, trying to mask the pain she felt inside. She wanted to be excited, to spend hours in the hangar bay, going over each function of the Phoenix. There was so much she had dreamed about doing when she got the chance to step foot in a Stellarnaut Atlas class. However, so much had changed in such a short time. Now, despite those long hours spent fantasizing about this exact moment, this exact place, she wanted nothing more than to track down Jaxson Blackwood and give him the same treatment he gave her family. It was all that she could think about.

"Do we get to stay in one of the bunks?" Lena asked. "I would love to see where my father stayed when he was stationed on this ship."

The look of pondering returned to Ryan's face. "Your father, huh? Well, as much as I would love to tell you that you will be staying with the crew, that is not the case," Ryan said. "Sadly, you'll have to stay in a cryopod."

Lena stopped in her tracks. "A cryopod?" she asked, hurt in her voice. "I can't go into cryosleep. I need to track down Blackwood for what he did to my family."

Ryan took in a deep breath. "I'm sorry, Lena, but if we don't do this, you'll be too old to take any action by the time we reach our next destination."

Lena thought about that for a moment, and then she asked: "Will I still be able to track Blackwood down?"

"Yes," Ryan said, though Lena detected doubt in his tone. "Blackwood should be in cryosleep as well if I had to guess." He paused for a moment as if he were thinking again. "Yes, I am sure of it. I doubt he has a Zephyr suit or anything similar."

"Is it safe?" she asked.

"Cryosleep is very safe, Lena," Arcturus answered. "That is what I was doing when you awakened me."

Lena looked at her friend and asked, "Are you going to do it too?"

"No," he answered. "There is no need for me to go into hibernation anymore. I have been awakened. It will do no good for me to sleep any longer. Due to my immortal lifespan, it would be ridiculous to waste time or energy on me."

"Immortal?" Lena asked. "I didn't know you were immortal."

"Most humans do not know," Arcturus said. "Now the two of you know. It is possible for my kind to be permanently shut down, but we do not age like your kind does. I believe Ryan Patel is a good person, and I felt it was okay to share the information with him as well."

Ryan looked at Arcturus, the compliment granting his curiosity and comfort to be exposed. "I'm sorry, I've been wondering this whole time; what are you, exactly, anyway?"

"I am Biotan," he answered.

"Biotan. Hmm," Ryan nodded. "I've heard of a Biotan; I've just never seen one before. You are definitely a unique-looking species, though. I would like to learn more about you and your people if you're comfortable with that." Ryan suddenly remembered something and returned to his busy-body demeanor. "Follow me, we're going to see Z. He's going to help us get you prepped for your..." He looked at Arcturus. "Hibernation. I've never heard cryosleep referred to as that before."

"Hibernation is a state of prolonged torpor or deep sleep," Arcturus responded, unaware that he'd just given Ryan the definition of an elementary word.

"I know what hibernation is," Ryan grinned and shook his head slightly as he walked. "Just never heard anyone use the word in place of 'cryosleep,' is all."

"Is it not the same?" Arcturus asked.

"I mean, kinda, but not really," Ryan answered. "There's a lot more to cryosleep than hibernation. In cryosleep, vitals have to be monitored at all times, the patient needs to be fed regularly, and they need to be hooked up to all these machines that help with that. Hibernation is just something some animals do. More self-sustaining. I guess that's applicable to a being who doesn't need to sleep in the first place, though. I suspect that you don't require a lot of the things most biological species do. It's contextual, then, I guess."

Arcturus just looked at Ryan for a moment as they walked. "Thank you for the clarification. The database I have on human language was slightly off on that subject."

"He doesn't need to eat, apparently," Lena added.

Ryan looked back at Arcturus, still at a brisk pace. "Huh?" he exclaimed. "No kidding?"

"No kidding?" Arcturus asked.

Lena and Ryan both smiled at each other. "I'll explain that one to you later; we're almost to Z." The two humans laughed, and the group continued to the cryo quarters.

They rounded a few more corners before Ryan spoke up. "When we get in here, don't be alarmed by Z's appearance. He's been through a lot in the past."

He opened a door, and they followed him in. There were two men on the other side of the room. One she recognized as

Dr. Kim, and the other, with his back to them, had two tubes sticking out of a device on his back and looping up over his shoulders. When he turned to see who had entered the room, it was apparent where the tubes were going. He had a mask over the lower portion of his face, with both tubes connected to the mask, one on each side of it. On the right side of his face was a steel plate that matched the contour of the left side. The plate covered all the way to his forehead, and over where his eye should have been was a white glow, like those within the Zephyr suits. The light didn't project out like a flashlight would; it simply shone on his face. The right side of his face seemed normal, and his Emerald-colored eye looked into both of Lena's. Lena felt as though she knew this person; he seemed so familiar, but she couldn't figure out how or why.

"Who do we have here, Patel?" the man said. His voice was raspy through the crackle of static emanating from the mask.

"This is Lena and Arcturus," Ryan said. "Lena, Arcturus, this is Z. He's the lead astro-technician on Ascendant 4, and he'll be in charge of overseeing your cryosleep."

"Lena," Z said in his static-laden voice, which off-put the girl. "Please come this way. Dr. Kim will need to take your vitals before we get started." He turned and walked across the room to a small opening on the side of the wall.

Lena turned to Ryan and whispered, "What happened to him? Why is his voice like that?" She was beginning to grow nervous. Her nerves had already been getting to her about the whole situation, to begin with, but now they were through the roof. She was frightened by how Z looked—by his whole demeanor, really—and she didn't know why. She'd never felt so scared of anyone like this before.

In a hushed voice, Ryan answered her, "It was before my time, but he was nearly killed in some battle years ago. Most likely because, at least, it's been said that he would never wear his Zephyr suit. The Stellarnauts have some of the most advanced doctors and astrotechs in the galaxy, and along with Maximilian Zephyr's technology, they were able to fix him up. But this is what we got out of it. The mask over his face has a built-in voice box. He can speak, but his mouth is messed up pretty badly. So, his speech is mostly incoherent, but the voice box allows us to understand him."

"Maximilian? I thought the captain was Janus Zephyr?" she asked.

Ryan raised an eyebrow, seeming surprised by Lena's confusion. "No, I'm talking about the leader of all the Stellarnauts. Captain Zephyr's father, Maximilian." Ryan hurriedly continued before Z could scold him. "Come on, they're waiting for you."

Shaking from her nerves, Lena walked over to where Dr. Kim, someone whom she had become comfortable with back on Zorath, was standing. She wished Z had come to Zorath; maybe she would have grown comfortable with him as well. But that probably wouldn't have made a difference because she had just met Ryan, and she was already very comfortable with him. There was something instinctual about Z.

*"Am I being judgmental because of the way he looks?"* she asked herself.

"What are you going to do?" Lena asked.

"I'm just going to get your vitals before you go into cryosleep. I am also going to draw a little blood to run some tests," Dr. Kim answered. "My name is Dr. Samuel Kim. I want to properly introduce myself."

"Samuel, I am Lena. Lena Zoravic," Lena said as she examined the room. "It's nice to meet you properly." She looked back at him. "I'm scared, Samuel."

"Don't be frightened," Z's voice came from her right. "I won't let anything happen to you."

Lena shivered as she looked over at the man. *"You're the main reason I'm scared,"* she thought to herself, too afraid to say those words aloud. That wasn't completely true, though. She was frightened about cryosleep itself, as well. She had read stories about some people who never woke up. It was apparently very rare and mostly affected the elderly, but the thought still scared her.

Lena felt Dr. Kim pull the band loose from her arm. "Okay, I have what I need. She's all yours, Z," he said. "I'll leave you to it." With that, the doctor left the room with several vials of Lena's blood.

Z was near a machine that had an opening at its front. Inside the opening was some padding that looked to be very comfortable to Lena. She was tired after the long day she had yesterday and the exhaustion from the trip up to this spacecraft. Walking all the way through the ship, she was ready to lie somewhere comfortable.

"Right over here, Miss Zoravic," Z pointed to the opening in the small chamber. "If you would just lie here, I'll get everything hooked up, and you can get some rest."

Lena went over to the chamber, Arcturus at her side. "Is there anything that I can assist with?" Arcturus asked Z.

"No, I can handle it," Z said. "You could go see if Patel needs any help."

"No, thank you. I will stay with Lena."

Z pulled several tubes and wires out of the side of the small chamber once Lena was inside. He started hooking the wires to her body, using small pads he stuck to her to attach the wires. "I'm going to give you an injection to help you sleep," Z said. He pulled out a small syringe and wrapped a band around her arm.

Lena looked at Arcturus and said, "I'm scared, Arcturus."

"Do not be frightened, Lena," Arcturus said. "I will be here to watch over you until the vow I made you came to fruition."

"Count to ten, please," Z said as he loosened the band.

"I will count with you," Arcturus said, placing his hand on her shoulder.

Lena reached up and took Arcturus's hand into hers. His hand was as soft as her mother's and as firm as her father's. She looked him in the eyes as they both started counting. "One, two, three, four..." Sleep took her. The fear she felt moments before faded. Not knowing why, she felt safe knowing Arcturus was there watching over her.

# Part 2

# Chapter 6

Ascendant 4

6252 ASST

Lena blinked her eyes open, her mind foggy. She looked around, attempting to wake herself up and recall where she was. "What is this place?" she asked herself. A man stood over her, and she could make out a green eye as she struggled to focus through the haze. It was as if she was blinded and was unable to make out what or who the image was. Her inner instinct could only think of one individual.

"Da... da..." She tried to say 'daddy,' but she struggled to get the word out. As she blinked, her vision cleared, revealing that she wasn't looking at her father.

"Lie still," came Z's raspy voice through a voice box attached to his face. Blinking her eyes to help focus better, she saw the mask-covered face of Z, the man who had hooked her up to all these tubes, looking down at her as he ran a scanner over her body. Tubes and wires were everywhere. As she scanned the room, trying to figure out what was going on, recognition took hold when she saw a robotic-looking being standing near her.

Raising her head proved to be futile. She realized that speaking wasn't even possible when she tried to ask what happened.

"You aren't strong enough to be trying to move about yet," she heard the voice of the young man who had escorted her here when she first arrived on the ship.

"He is correct," came the friendly voice she remembered from the cave back in Zorath. As she recalled the cave, memories flooded back, and she pieced together what had happened before she left home and why she was now with the Stellarnauts. *Mommy, Daddy... Kian,* she thought as tears welled up in her eyes.

"Her vitals look good," Z said once he finished his scan.

"Lena? Are you okay?" Arcturus asked, concern evident as tears started rolling down her cheeks.

Her head was gently pushed back down to its resting position and held in place. "This is going to be much easier if you lie still," Z said. "Patel, get the wheelchair."

Ryan went across the room and pushed a wheeled chair over to where they were unhooking all the wires and tubes from Lena's body. Once everything was completely removed, Z reached under Lena's back and lifted her. He didn't look like he would be strong enough to lift a full-grown person, but he managed with relative ease. A couple of steps later, he gently lowered her into the wheelchair.

"Take her to her quarters and have her cleaned and fed. Then, get her to Lieutenant Johnson for physical therapy. If she's going to wear that suit you two have been altering, she'll need to learn to walk again."

"Absolutely, walking will be vital too, especially while wearing the suit," Arcturus said as he and Ryan wheeled Lena from the cryo-chamber.

"Arr…" Lena tried to say Arcturus' name. She rolled her head around, trying to stretch the muscles in her neck and shoulders.

"Lena, give your body and mind time to get accustomed to being woken from cryosleep," Ryan said reassuringly. "In time, you'll be able to speak normally. Your mind and body have been shut down for nearly twenty-five years."

Lena's eyes opened wide, fixed on Ryan with intensity. "Twen…" Still unable to articulate the words, her body language conveyed her shock and disbelief.

"Yes, it's been twenty-five years since we put you under," Ryan confirmed.

"Lena, it was necessary for you to sleep for so long," Arcturus reassured her. "Otherwise, you would have been too old to fulfill your destiny."

*Fulfill my destiny? What is he going on about now?* she thought to herself, knowing she wouldn't be able to ask him right now.

"However, you must not fear cryosleep any longer," Arcturus said, holding up a finger as he spoke. "Ryan and I have altered an old..."

"Arcturus," Ryan interrupted. "It's supposed to be a secret."

Arcturus had an apologetic look on his face, no doubt realizing he had almost ruined their surprise. Lena looked between the two of them as they rounded a corner and nearly ran into Captain Zephyr, who was accompanied by another young Stellarnaut soldier. The Stellarnaut was a young woman who appeared to be of the same ethnicity as Dr. Kim. She held a device across her left forearm that looked similar to the handheld game system Kian would often walk around their house playing on. The woman was looking down at the device and had a small pointing apparatus in her opposite hand, poking at the screen as they walked toward them.

"They've spotted the Rogue again," the young lady was saying as they approached the three of them. "He's near the Ci'gar System, possibly making his way to Voltorin."

"Ci'gar is my brother's sector," Captain Zephyr said. "This Rogue is Orion's problem for now. If he comes back to New Andromeda, then we'll deal with him then."

"Do you think he could be trying to get to the Sol System?" the young Stellarnaut woman said. "Possibly try to confront your father for whatever reason?"

As the captain and his companion approached them, the captain said, "Chen, we'll continue this discussion another time. We have company." He then turned his attention to Ryan and said, "Patel, Arcturus, and Leya, I see you're awake," addressing the small group.

"Her name is Lena," Arcturus corrected.

"Yes, it's been a while, Lena." Zephyr shot her a knowing grin." "How are you feeling?" He asked.

Knowing she wouldn't be able to answer, Lena looked to Ryan. "She's just been pulled from the cryo-chamber, Captain Zephyr. We're going to get her fed, then escort her to Lieutenant Johnson ~~now~~ for physical therapy."

"Carry on," Captain Zephyr replied to Ryan's statement. They continued past them, and then the captain stopped, turned back towards them, and asked, "What can you tell me about the inhabitants of the planet Nivaria, Patel?"

Knowing she'd read all about the Nivarians, Lena started squirming in her seat. Her eyes pierced the captain as she tried to speak, "Frr..." That was all she was able to get out of the word friendly. She knew much more about the Nivarian people than just that.

"Do you know about them?" the captain asked directly. Lena nodded, then reached up to her throat and tried to clear it. Captain Zephyr looked up at Ryan and said, "Once she's back on her feet and talking, please inform me, Patel."

"Yes sir," Ryan said, standing with his back straightened and saluting his captain. He then loosened his posture and continued, "I'm certain Arcturus will also be coming along. He hasn't left her side for the nearly twenty-five years she's been resting."

"Has it been twenty-five years already?" the captain asked. "Her rescue is the only non-combat landing that stands out in my head, mostly due to the fact that it was the death of my old friend." Lena's face lowered, tears welling again. "I am sorry, Lena. I forgot that this is still fresh to you due to cryosleep. I am not normally that insensitive."

Looking back into his eyes, she nodded, then glanced back up at Arcturus and Ryan. They turned and pushed her down the hall and into the hell she would know as therapy for the next few weeks.

Lieutenant Jake Johnson was a ruthless therapist. He didn't cut the small, petite Lena any slack; she was treated just as a big, muscled man would have been. His methods were effective, though; Lena was on her feet, walking the rail before the end of her second session.

Lena's voice was back near the end of day one; after a few drinks of water and a meal, she was able to speak again, though it was still hard and hurt her throat.

When Lena wheeled into the therapy room for the fifth consecutive day, she looked Lieutenant Johnson straight in the eyes and declared, "I'm ready." Knowing she wasn't, knowing her muscle throbbed from the pain of going through the motions yesterday and the days prior. However, she didn't want to give him the satisfaction of thinking he'd beat her down.

"Good," the giant, muscled man with dark skin said. "Today, we walk without the rail." His accent was unlike anyone else she'd met on this ship, although she hadn't met many people thus far.

"Without the rail?" Lena complained. "I know I'm getting better, but do you really think I'm ready to walk unassisted already?"

"Yesterday, you did well," Lieutenant Johnson said. "Today, you will do even better. I have faith in you."

"He was right; she had worked hard. By the end of the session, she managed to take three steps without using the rail. Breathing heavily, she looked up from her bent position in the wheelchair and met the lieutenant's gaze, "Thank you," she said. The look on his face conveyed confusion. "For pushing me; you had faith in me, and now I have faith in myself as well. For tomorrow's session, I will get out of this chair. I know I can do it, and I will prove it."

The lieutenant chuckled, "We'll see."

The next day was similar to the day before, with the exception that Lena walked far more than three steps unsupported.

She and the lieutenant were getting along nicely. Despite his imposing appearance, resembling someone who could snap her in two, he was remarkably gentle. He was pushy, unforgiving, and determined in his work with her, but Lena could tell he was genuinely a good person. It was evident that this man loved his work; he enjoyed giving people the encouragement they needed to overcome their fears and disabilities. Not thinking she was disabled, but had he not been there to push her and give her the proper motivation, she feared she may still be sitting in that damned chair.

After her therapy session at the end of the second week, Captain Zephyr came to see her. Arcturus was at her side as always, other than during physical therapy. He was very protective of her. Lena hadn't really noticed it at first, but as the days went by after she woke up, she realized he wouldn't let her out of his sight. *I'll have to ask him about why he's like that with me,* she thought.

The captain walked into the room. He nodded toward Arcturus and said, "Arcturus, how have you been?"

"I have been well, thank you, Captain Janus Zephyr," Arcturus replied.

He then turned his attention to Lena. "Lena Zoravic, how have you been? Johnson speaks highly of you. He hasn't released a patient a week earlier in many years."

"I'm coming along," she said. "Lieutenant Johnson was very determined to get me walking and talking again. I think he regrets the talking part, though," she laughed at her attempt at humor.

"Yeah, Johnson enjoys peace and quiet," the captain said with a chuckle. "I hope you didn't fill his head with too much teenage nonsense."

Captain Zephyr also laughed at his own attempt at a joke.

Lena chuckled, "No, we mostly talked about the work we were doing, and I asked a lot of questions, maybe too many now that I think about it."

"He will be fine," the captain said reassuringly. "You have done well. You're back on your feet quicker than I thought."

"Thank you!" Lena said proudly.

He just nodded at her in acknowledgment of her thanks. "Your therapy sessions aren't why I made my visit today." He turned to the door and said, "Chen, please come in."

The young woman whom Lena had seen with the captain a few weeks ago came through the door. She was a small woman with a light brown skin tone, her eyes dark brown, bearing a look as though she could kill someone. Her Zephyr suit was a dark gray, almost black. If Captain Zephyr hadn't been there with his black suit on, Lena would have thought it to be black. The suit had brown accents where Captain Zephyr's had silver, and it had the word "Zephyr" etched in the upper right chest plate, just like each suit she'd seen prior.

"This is Specialist Emily Chen. She is my master of intelligence. I have her here to take notes on our conversation." The captain turned his attention from Lena to Specialist Chen.

Chen inclined her head ever so slightly, never taking her eyes from Lena's. " We would like to know what information you have on the Nivarian species. And how is it that a girl from a remote planet in the middle of nowhere knows about them?" She maintained her unwavering gaze on Lena, who, in return, didn't flinch from the small woman's glare.

"Well, if you must know," Lena said, turning to grab the bag she'd brought aboard the ship and reaching inside.

Before she could bring out the book she was reaching for, Specialist Chen reached to her side and swiftly drew a sidearm that Lena hadn't even seen on her hip at the woman's side and aimed it at her.

"Take your hand from the bag slowly."

Arcturus stepped between Lena and Chen. "You may not eliminate Lena."

"Step aside, Arcturus," Lena said as she looked from the weapon to Captain Zephyr. "It's just a book," she said, pulling a book from the bag and holding it up for Emily to see. "My mother gave them to me. She was old school like that, preferring the feel of the pages in her hand versus the glare of a screen when she read. My father would get the books when he went to the traders' bazaars that would come to Zorath's orbit from time to time."

"Lower your weapon, Chen, and don't draw it aboard my ship again without my order," Captain Zephyr said, reaching for the book. Lena handed it to him, and he examined the covers, front and back, ~~of the book~~. "Do you not realize these books have been banned by Emperor Kraytus Sivik nearly a thousand years ago? How did Darian get his hands on one?"

Lena looked at the captain. "Banned?" she asked, not addressing anyone in particular. "Why would my mother and father want books that were banned by the emperor?" Again, her words seemed directed more to herself than to anyone else.

"I spent ten years undercover on Emperor Sivik's Titan, and there were no copies of these books to be found," Chen stated.

"The fact that a sniveling little Zorathain brat like yourself has one is very suspicious to me."

Lena reached into her bag and pulled out the other one she had. "Well, I have two of the four of them. How suspicious is that?" she asked.

Chen grabbed the book from Lena's hands and examined it, opening it and flipping through the pages. "Captain, do you realize the information we can get from these books? I can't believe I'm holding one of the four books on alien history." She reached over and grabbed the book from the captain's hand, "Now I hold two of them."

Lena leaned forward and took the books from Chen, and said, "Well, they're mine. If you want to read them, you're going to have to be nicer." She tucked the second book back inside her bag and opened the first one; she pulled out to the page that said, *"Nivarian."*

*Nivarian: A race of tall, slender beings with iridescent skin and long, pointed ears. They possess powerful telekinetic abilities and are known for their deep connection to the planet's natural energy. It is believed that their telekinesis is tied to the planet's core.*

*It is known that if Nivarians are removed from their home planet and the connection to the planet's energy is lost, they will wither away and die very rapidly.*

*Their telekinetic ability is one of the most unique abilities we've encountered on our journeys. However, their inability to leave the planet without risking death makes it very difficult to study their ability.*

*They are a very friendly and non-hostile species, possessing extensive knowledge of their planet and the energy that grants them their telekinetic ability.*

"Reading through this, it looks to me like they are very friendly, something I tried to tell you when I was first woken up," Lena said, looking up from the book. "It also says they have telekinesis, an ability they inherited from their planet's core energy. I also am friendly and non-hostile!"

Captain Zephyr stepped forward and asked, "Could I borrow your book so I can read up on this species?"

"Hesitantly, Lena folded the book closed, held it close to her chest, and then asked, "Why do you need to know about the Nivarian anyway?"

"We are nearing their planet, and I personally make it a priority to learn everything I can about a planet's inhabitants before I land on the surface," Captain Zephyr explained.

Lena's eyes opened wide. This was her opportunity; she could explore an alien planet. Something she had dreamed of since she was able to explore her home planet on her own.

"These books are very dear to me; as I said before, they were gifts from my parents. I'll let you borrow them on one condition," she said. "You have to let me accompany you when you go to Navaria."

"Absolutely not," the captain said without hesitation.

"Why not?" Lena protested.

"First off, you just learned to walk again. Secondly, you've never been anywhere other than Zorath; therefore, we don't know how this planet's gravity will affect you. Thirdly, and probably most importantly of all, you're not a Stellarnaut, and you don't have a Zephyr suit."

"She has done well with her strength," Arcturus said. "If she does have a Zephyr suit, the gravity wouldn't be an issue, am I correct?"

"Well, technically, yes," Captain Zephyr said. "But I only brought up the gravity thing because she doesn't have a suit."

"She does," Arcturus said.

"What?" Zephyr asked simultaneously with Lena, both of them looking at Arcturus.

"Ryan and myself have been working on an old Zephyr suit he found in a storage unit," Arcturus said. "We have made a few adjustments, allowing it to hopefully adapt to her."

"That's impossible," Zephyr said. "Every Zephyr suit is genetically tailored to the wearer. She has never been through the Stellarnaut Academy; therefore, she doesn't have a suit tailored to her."

"Ryan believes the suit belonged to her father," Arcturus said. "When he found it, the name D. Zoravic was engraved on the inside collar of the armor."

"My father's?" Lena asked, stunned. "You and Ryan have been tailoring my father's old suit to fit my genetics?"

"It was Ryan who came up with the suit and the idea. I merely helped you alter the suit. Ryan has been a huge help, though," Arcturus explained.

Tears welled in Lena's eyes again. She couldn't believe what she was hearing. Ryan Patel and Arcturus, two people she barely knew, were doing this for her. It was beyond belief.

How had they been able to do such a thing without the captain knowing? She looked up at the captain, tears still in her eyes. "Please let me have the suit and go with you all to this new planet."

Zephyr's head dropped as he contemplated his decision. "If I allow this, you are not to leave my side."

"Nor mine," Arcturus chimed in.

"Yes, you're going too," the captain said to Arcturus. "I'll need you to help me keep her in line. I don't have the same trust in her that I do for my crew."

"Are you seriously going to let this little girl accompany you to the surface of a planet we ourselves have never been to?" Chen asked, frustration evident in her voice.

"She is Darian Zoravic's kid," Zephyr responded. "What could go wrong?" He laughed, then turned and walked from the room. Emily Chen lectured the captain about his decision as far as Lena could hear them as they walked down the hall.

Lena turned her attention to Arcturus, got to her feet, walked over to him, and wrapped her arms around his neck. "Thank you! Could we go find Ryan so I can thank him too and see my suit?"

# Chapter 7

Ascendant 4

6252 ASST

Ryan was in the training room down the hall from the barracks. He was fully geared up in his Zephyr suit, along with armor, and wearing standard gray armor with black accents.

"Lena!" Ryan said excitedly. Then, seeming to realize he may have been a little too ambitious seeing her, he said, "I mean, hey Lena, how are you?" He turned his attention to Arcturus, nodding his head to the strange being, and said, "Arcturus, how are you?" His demeanor changed to a more serious one.

Lena noticed multiple soldiers in the training room, most of them engaged in intensive training exercises. Each one of them was wearing armored Zephyr suits. These suits, combined with the armor, granted the Stellarnaut soldiers a huge advantage in combat. It made sense for them to train fully geared up, enabling them to take full advantage of all the suit had to offer.

Built-in thrusters were one of the many features Lena noticed them training with. It was amazing how easily one could get back to their feet if knocked to the ground or redirect their movements in another direction. A few were training with swords that looked as though they came straight out from under the armor of the wielder's forearm. These weren't typical swords like those made from steel back on Zorath. No, these were made of a bright white glow, the same white glow that emanated from the seams in the armor.

"I am doing well, Ryan," Arcturus responded.

"What are they training with there?" Lena asked Ryan, gesturing to the weapons.

Ryan turned to where she was pointing. "Those are ether-lumina blades," he answered without hesitation. "Not all Zephyr suits are equipped with them, but I've always wanted one. They're pretty cool and can cut through anything except another ether-lumina blade and most Zephyr suits."

"Why don't you have one?" Lena asked him.

One of the soldiers was knocked back and nearly ran through the three of them as they stood there talking. The soldier kicked his feet and palms back, then engaged his thrusters, slowing himself enough to redirect back to his battle, and lunged back at his foe.

"Let's move over here," Ryan said, stepping away from the immediate danger of flying Stellernauts. Lena and Arcturus followed. "I'm an Astrotech, we don't," he emphasized the word 'don't' by using his finger to make quotes beside his head, "need them," he continued, "Captain Zephyr claims. He says only field soldiers require them. Apparently, they're difficult to install, and a lot of ether-lumina is used to power them. That's why most field soldiers have the larger power packs on their backs."

"Ryan, I'm going to need you to assume that I've lived on a small planet called Zorath for the first sixteen years of my life and then spent all the rest of my life aboard this ship in cryosleep," Lena said. "Oh, and let's pretend I have no clue what ether-lumina is."

"I'm sorry, Lena," Ryan said. "I'm just so used to being around Stellarnaut soldiers who all know as much as I do or even more. Ether-lumina is a power source created by Maximilian Zephyr. It is what powers all the Stellarnaut ships and Zephyr suits. It's the white glow you see coming from within the suit, Phoenix's, this ship, hell; it's even the white glow in Z's mask."

"That is correct," Arcturus said. "According to what I have learned since aboard this vessel, Maximilian Zephyr has much to do with how the Stellarnauts run." Arcturus gestured to the glow at his chest. "It appears to me that the ether-lumina power source and my power source are similar in some ways. I have studied the power sources extensively over the years that I have been here."

"That's very interesting, Arcturus," Ryan said. "Just as interesting as it was the last fifty times you told me about it." Ryan turned to walk across the room. "Come on, Lena, let's get you outfitted. I'd like to see if the work Arcturus and I put into this suit has been worth it. Your dad's old suit was outdated and in bad condition, but we've made a few minor adjustments, and I believe they will suit your needs for a Zephyr suit just fine."

"Just the fact that you were able to find my dad's old suit is suitable enough for me," Lena said as they walked across the room. Looking around, she saw a pair across the room training in hand-to-hand combat. "Is there a trainer here? Someone to help a recruit learn the basics of combat?"

"Yeah," Ryan said. "I was going to introduce you to someone once we got you geared up."

"I think Riddick Shaw will be the perfect trainer for you; he's patient and very good at what he does. You'll have to be patient with him, too, though. He doesn't speak, so he's kinda hard to work with. But if memory serves me correctly, he was your father's trainer as well. It would be excellent because you can learn to be as capable as your father if you follow his ways," Ryan explained.

"Yeah, you're going to need some training, Zorthian," a familiar voice came from behind her. Lena turned to see Emily Chen standing in the middle of the training floor. "Your first lesson is on me."

She started walking toward Lena. Lena, in turn, decided she would show her what a Zorthian native was capable of when it came to self-defense and started walking in Emily's direction.

"What is your deal with me, Chen?" Lena asked as she approached the woman.

Emily didn't give her the satisfaction of an answer. Once they were close enough to engage in combat, Emily swung her right arm, hitting Lena in the side of the face. Disoriented, Lena tried to turn back to where Chen was, but she was gone. Pain in her lower back came from nowhere, knocking her to the ground. Then Emily's weight was upon her. With a knee in her back, Lena screamed at the pressure Emily was putting on the small of her back. Emily grabbed her by the back of the hair and pulled her face off the ground. She leaned in and whispered into her ear. "Watch your back; you never know where I'll be." Then Emily slammed Lena's face against the floor and got off her back. She turned to walk from the room.

"Emily Chen," Arcturus's voice came from above Lena. "You must also watch your back. Do not forget Arcturus is aboard this vessel as well." He then bent over to help Lena to her feet.

Emily turned back around and asked, "Did you just threaten me, you freak?"

Looking up from his knelt position, Arcturus replied, "I did not. I merely stated the fact that I, too, was aboard this vessel and that your back should be watched just as Lena's must be." He then reached out and rolled his hand into a fist very slowly as though he was gesturing for her to come to him. Not able to see beyond Arcturus, Lena couldn't see Emily. Arcturus could say things that may be misunderstood, but he meant them well. Emily just had to see his sincerity.

Emily made a scoffing sound before turning to walk away. When she did turn, Lena heard a crashing sound and then laughter amongst the other soldiers. Wiping her watery eyes, Lena could see Emily lying across a cart that had a viewing monitor on it.

Emily got to her feet and said to the soldiers in the room, "I am your superior officer; show a little more respect." The laughter died down as Emily Chen left the training room.

"I did warn her to watch her back as well," Arcturus said as he bent over to help Lena to her feet.

Ryan stepped over and helped Arcturus pull Lena to her feet. "What was that all about?" He asked.

"Chen doesn't like me," Lena said. "She thinks I'm a spy from Zorath or something. I can't stand her. I don't know why she feels that way. I have already been through so much."

"Well, it is apparent she doesn't like you. Don't worry about it for now," Ryan said. "Either way, we need to get you suited up."

"I'm not in the mood anymore," Lena said. "I just want to go back to my room and lie down. I need some time to think, please."

"That is not an option right now," Ryan said firmly. "You have to get the suit on. It will make you feel better. Trust me."

Sighing, Lena replied, "I really do appreciate everything, Ryan, but I don't even think I could right now. My back is so sore, and my face is killing me. My body will thank you if you let me rest."

Arcturus grabbed Lena by the head and began examining her face. "Your face does not appear to be killing you. It is, however, very bloody and bruised."

Lena smiled at her odd, robotic friend. "It's just a figure of speech. My face isn't literally killing me; I mean, it just hurts really badly, and I don't feel like dealing with the suit right now. What do I do!"

"Thank you for the clarification," Arcturus said. "That being the case, I believe Ryan Patel is correct. The suit will make you feel better. Wear it, and you will see."

They continued across the training room and entered a dressing room. There were more soldiers here getting geared up for their own training sessions. Ryan walked over to a locker that had the word "Zoravic" written on the door. "Your combination code is 6227," he whispered as he started punching buttons on the door of the locker. "It's the year we picked you up; I figured it would be easy for you to remember."

He opened the locker, reached in, and pulled out a small, light gray bodysuit. He handed the suit to her and said, "Arcturus can assist you if you need help. I will be out here. Let me know once you have this portion on, and I can assist with the armor." He then stepped back and pulled a curtain around in front of her locker.

She turned and looked at Arcturus, "Could you please leave too? I would like to get myself dressed alone."

Arcturus nodded and stepped back to the other side of the curtain. "She said she would like to get herself dressed," he said to Ryan once he was on the other side of the curtain.

"I heard her," Ryan replied. "These," he must have gestured at the curtain because it rustled a bit, "don't restrict sound very well."

Lena smiled to herself. Despite the pain she was in, she couldn't help but enjoy her two new friends. She sat down on a bench and examined the suit Ryan had handed her. The words *"D. Zoravic"* were stretched in the fabric of the suit. While pulling it into her chest, tears started swelling in her eyes once again. "I miss you, Daddy." The fabric of the suit looked like small wiring woven together. It was a very interesting-looking suit, and it didn't seem to fit her properly. "Ryan," she said, trying to get his attention. The curtain started to rustle again. "Don't come in here. I just don't think this thing is going to fit me, and I honestly don't think it would have fit my dad. He was a lot bulkier than I will ever be."

The curtains stopped moving, and Ryan said, "I'm sorry, I wasn't trying to come in while you were changing. I just thought you needed me."

"It's fine," she said. "I just really don't think this thing will fit me."

"The suit is designed to mold itself to your body," Ryan said reassuringly. "Once you start putting it on, it will adjust its size to fit you."

"Really?" she questioned, holding the suit up and examining it. "Guess I need to get this done," she thought. Standing, she started to undress. It was very painful getting her clothes off and looking in a mirror inside her locker, she could see her back had a huge bruise on it where Emily Chen had kneed her. *Let's see if Ryan is right. Hopefully, this thing does fit me. I don't think I could get my pants back on right now,* she thought.

Stepping into the leggings of the suit, she pulled it up surprisingly easily. The suit did adjust itself to fit her perfectly. She didn't know how it worked, but it felt amazing against her skin. Once she pulled the rest of the suit over her shoulders, it started to emit a glow, that same white glow that illuminated the rest of the Zephyrs she'd seen since she had first come in contact with the Stellarnauts.

"Ryan, Arcturus," she said. "Something is happening. I need you to come in here."

Ryan and Arcturus both pulled the curtain aside and stepped into where she was. Lena was kneeling, unable to hold herself upright. The suit was doing something to her, something she couldn't explain.

"What is wrong?" Arcturus asked.

"I don't know, but it feels like the suit is tingling," Lena said. "It is pulsing throughout my whole body. The feeling is making it hard to stand."

"That's normal," Ryan said. "It will feel very strange at first, especially considering this is the first time you're ever wearing a Zephyr suit. It is getting itself acquainted with you while at the same time repairing the damages you sustained during your encounter with Chen. You will eventually get used to that feeling, and it won't cause you to lose your composure."

The sensation of the suit was running through her entire body, not just over her skin.

As Lena wore the suit, she felt pulsing deep inside, spreading throughout her entire body. After a few minutes, the pain she was feeling prior to putting it on was dissipating. It felt amazing wearing this suit; she felt as though she were in a new body, and this body was indestructible. Rolling her neck around on her shoulders, she exclaimed, "I feel great! I can't believe how well or how fast that happened." Holding her arms out in front of her, she could see all the woven wires pulsating over her skin. It was faint but noticeable. "What's next?" she asked, taking her eyes from the suit and looking Ryan in the eyes.

"Next," he said, walking to the locker with a huge smile on his face. It was clear he was happy with himself for making this a reality for her. "Next, we make sure the armor adheres to the suit correctly. Each piece of armor is separate, and the suit itself holds it in place." He demonstrated by reaching up and pulling one of the pauldrons from his shoulder and examining it. He held it up for her to see. "Now all I have to do is place it back over the suit, and it takes hold of the piece and stays there to protect me if the need arises."

Inside the locker, there was a huge assortment of armor pieces. Ryan reached in and grabbed a shoulder pauldron, tossing it to Lena. She caught it, something she wasn't completely sure she would have been able to do before. Considering he didn't exactly toss it directly at her, almost deliberately throwing it out of her reach, she somehow managed to maneuver herself in a way to catch it. It was surprisingly lightweight, much lighter than she would have thought it to be.

"Wow!" she exclaimed. "I think this suit makes me more agile, too?" she questioned.

"It does," Ryan confirmed. "I was hoping you'd catch on to that on your own. The suit enhances all sorts of abilities."

Lena followed Ryan's example and placed the pauldron over her shoulder. The suit almost grabbed it from her hand and pulled it to her shoulder, where it stayed in place. She reached up to pull it away, and it came right off, then placed it back where it belonged. She repeated this a few more times before Ryan spoke up again.

He stepped closer to her and asked, "Do you mind?" As he reached for the pauldron, Lena looked him in the eye and said, "Okay, what are you doing?"

"I'm going to attempt to pull the armor from your suit," Ryan explained.

"Oh, okay, yeah," Lena replied.

Ryan reached up, took hold of the shoulder piece, and pulled on it. It didn't move. He pulled harder; this time, Lena moved toward him, but the armor stayed in place.

"Only the wearer of the suit can remove armor from it. No one else can take the armor from your body. Unless you're dead, then the suit has no reason to hold the armor in place any longer," Ryan explained.

Over the next several minutes, Ryan and Arcturus explained the different armor pieces to Lena, where they went, and their uses. Once Lena was completely geared up, she didn't think she would be able to move because of all the added friction this armor would cause.

Getting to her feet after adding the final leg greaves, Lena couldn't believe how easy it was for her to move normally. "The design of this suit is amazing," she said. "It's so much easier to move than I thought it would be."

"From the understanding I have acquired during my studies," Arcturus said, "the Zephyr suit enhances numerous bodily functions."

"That's right," Ryan confirmed. "Agility, strength, reaction timing, even one's ability to continue fighting if all hope is lost. And I've equipped your suit with OmniSight; it's a scanning device that allows you to scan objects or beings, and it displays a brief description on your ArmComm."

"What's an OmniSight and ArmComm?" Lena asked.

"An OmniSight is what I said before exactly, a device for scanning stuff, and your ArmComm is the display HUD on your wrist armor. It's used for communications, gathering, and sending information."

Lena reached out with her left arm to scan Arcturus. "How does it work?" she asked.

"It's really," Ryan said, "All you have to do is think about what you want to scan, and it will scan it."

Lena thought about scanning Arcturus. Her palm lit up for a second, and then a display showed up on the small screen on her forearm. It read:

*Biotan: Discovered in 54 ASST by renowned scientist Maximilian Zephyr.Home Planet: Ascendant-2.*

*Domain: N/A Kingdom: N/APhylum: N/A Class: N/A*

*Order: N/A*

*Suborder: N/A*

*Infraorder: N/A*

*Physical Description: Bipedal humanoids. Appears almost mechanical.*

*Average weight: N/A*

*Average height: N/A*

*Skin color: Silvery-gray with a metallic shine*

*Eye color: White with a black pupil*

*Editor's Note: Much more information has not been gathered on the Biotans.*

*Shortly after the discovery, they have gone missing and have not been seen since.*

It displayed the same data on Biotans that her book on alien species gave.

"I hope you do not mind," Arcturus said. "I took it upon myself to add the data from your books to your ArmComm."

Lena looked up at him. "You went through my bag?" she asked him.

"I did," Arcturus responded, with no hesitation or indication that he'd done anything wrong.

"Arcturus!" Lena exclaimed. "You can't rummage through other people's belongings without their permission."

"Oh," Arcturus seemed confused by this statement. He turned to Ryan and asked, "Did you know about this, Ryan Patel?"

"Yeah, I wouldn't have gone through Lena's stuff without her knowing," Ryan answered.

"How is it that you came to find Darian Zoravic's Zephyr suit?" He asked. "If not for you going through items that do not belong to you?"

Ryan flushed. "I see where that could be taken wrong, but I was doing my job. You see, we were slow in the lab for a while, so Z had me going through old storage crates…" he hesitated for a second as though he were thinking about what to say. "I was looking for old parts," he settled on as his lie.

"Regardless," Lena interrupted. "Arcturus, thank you for entering the data. Moving forward, please don't go through my things."

Arcturus nodded his head. "I understand," he said before he started making the same gesture he did back on Zorath. He stood with his right hand up, and he started making the hand gesture…

Lena interrupted him. "Arcturus, you don't have to make a vow every time I ask you to do something. As my friend, I believe that if you tell me you won't do it, then you won't do it. That's what friends do; they trust each other. Hello friend!"

Arcturus lowered his hand. "You will trust my word?" he asked. "As friends, we trust each other without a vow to do so?"

"Yes, Arcturus," Lena said, looking him in the eyes. "We are friends. I trust that you will respect my privacy, and I will respect yours in turn. Let's high-five!"

The shock in Arcturus's face showed it all. He had never

had a true friend before, someone whom he could count on at any given time. "Thank you, Lena," he said. "It is a true honor to be your friend."

"How do I high-five? What is that?"

"Just raise your hand and meet my hand as I move it toward you, like a clap." They both high-fived.

"See. It was easy, wasn't it?"

"Yes, most certainly. It was easy and fun, too! Let's do it again!"

They both high-fived again. Lena nodded to him, then turned to Ryan. "That goes for you too. If we're going to be friends, we have to trust each other."

"Okay," Ryan said. "But I had nothing to do with him going through your bag."

Lena nodded her head as they went back to going over the functions of the suit. She noticed a slot in the armor on her thigh; there wasn't one in Ryan's armor. "What's this for?" she asked, pointing at the slot.

"Oh," Ryan said excitedly. "I almost forgot." He walked over to a locker that said Patel on the door and punched in a code.

"What's your code?" Lena asked.

Ryan just turned and looked at her as though she had just asked for his soul. "I'm not telling you the code to my locker; that's my personal stuff in there."

"You know my code," she said.

"Yeah, because I made it up for you. You can change it at any time. All that talk about trust, and you want to go through my locker," Ryan laughed.

"Oh," she said. "I didn't know I could change it, sorry. And for the record, I wouldn't have gone through your locker."

He turned back to the locker and opened the door; reaching inside, he grabbed something and then shut the door. Once he got back over to her, he reached out and handed her the revolver that she picked up after everything happened on Zorath. Holding the weapon in her hands brought memories of that day. She fought back the urge to cry.

"This should slip down into its holster on your leg," Ryan said. He also had a small crate in his other hand; he held it out to her. "You only had four bullets, so I took it upon myself to engineer some advanced bullets for your weapon. I hope they work."

Lena slid the revolver into the slot at her hip, and it was a perfect fit. She took the crate, opened the lid, and looked inside. It had several smaller boxes inside it. Each box was labeled pulse, concussion, grav, laser, and original.

"Each bullet has its own unique function," Ryan said. "The pulse, concussion, and grav bullets are non-lethal. The laser bullet shoots a beam of ether-lumina that will cut through just about anything. And the box that says original contains the four bullets that were in the gun when it arrived."

Lena pulled out one of the laser bullets and examined it. There was a swirl of white energy in the tip. She looked over at Arcturus and saw the same white swirl in his chest. She put the bullet back in its container, turned toward the door, and said, "Now let's go find this trainer and see what this suit can do."

# Chapter 8

## Ascendant 4

## 6552 ASST

When they re-entered the training room, Ryan walked over to a man who wasn't much larger than him. The larger Stellarnaut wore a blue Zephyr suit with black accents. Like all the suits, it had the signature glowing white seams and joints powered by ether-lumina, as Ryan explained.

After talking to the man for a few moments, Ryan turned and motioned for Lena and Arcturus to come over to them.

"Lena, I would like you to meet Riddick Shaw," Ryan said as she approached. "Riddick, this is Lena Zoravic, Darian Zoravic's daughter."

Riddick stood there with his hands behind his back, nodding to Lena. He then turned his attention to Arcturus, who was coming up behind Lena. Riddick inclined his head toward him as well, but he did not speak.

"Riddick Shaw," Arcturus greeted the large man. "Nice to see you again. Ryan Patel told Lena you would be an excellent trainer for her due to her inexperience in combat training."

"Thank you, Arcturus," Lena said, embarrassed. "You don't have to blab my business to everyone."

"Yes, thank you, Arcturus," Ryan said, glancing at Lena. "You don't have to worry about Riddick saying anything to anyone." He turned back to Riddick and said, "As our friend here said, Lena has never had any combat training at all, and I believe you to be the best candidate to show her the ropes."

Riddick used his head to gesture for Lena to step into the middle of the training area. Not knowing what else to do but follow, she found herself face-to-face, or rather face-to-chest, with Riddick. He then brought his hands from behind his back, bent his knees slightly, and put his hands out in front of himself. He stood there in the fighting stance, then nodded his head to her.

Confused as to why he wasn't explaining to her what to do, she did as he had. She bent her knees slightly and brought her hands out in front of her. Riddick looked her up and down, then walked over and placed his hand below her left elbow, lifting it ever so gently to a point before stopping. This positioned her left-hand near level with the bottom of her chin. Once he had her arms where he wanted them, he pulled her right leg back slightly and then bent her left leg a bit more. Then he used his right hand to swing around as though to hit her in the face. Lena reacted with her left arm, able to bring her hand up quickly enough to block him from landing the blow.

Riddick nodded and then reached over to adjust her right arm down just a little. He then used his right arm to swing at her again, and she, in turn, lifted her left arm to block. Riddick then nodded toward her right arm and gestured with his head. She interpreted this as him wanting her to use it to swing. Lena looked at him, then to her hand, then back to him, and finally swung her arm towards him. In response, Riddick used his left arm to deflect her attempt to hit him.

They went back and forth like that for a few moments. Riddick involved some other part of her to use in her attacks and defenses. Within about an hour, she and Riddick were sparring back and forth. Lena stepped forward to swing, then raised her left arm to block, then her right arm to block another attempt at her face. In response, she swung her left arm at Riddick's stomach, where he used his right arm to block. She then swung with her right arm at his head, which was also blocked.

Riddick stepped back and placed his hands together, his left hand forming a fist while his right hand pushed against it with its palm. He bent forward at the waist just a little in a bow, then turned and walked to the wall on the right side of the room. There, he picked up a pen and wrote on a piece of paper pinned there. Once he was done, Lena, Arcturus, and Ryan walked over to see what he'd written.

Under his name he penciled Lena's name beneath his own, with the word "daily" and the time "0500" written next to that.

"That's good," Ryan said.

"What's good?" Lena asked.

"Riddick has accepted you as a student," Ryan answered. "He saw something in you during your first session. Most trainers want to give you a few beginner lessons before they accept a student. Not every trainer is for every student."

"Well, that is good," Lena said, obviously happy with herself. "But, I do have one question. Why didn't he speak to me during the session?"

"I didn't want to say anything prior to you meeting him and getting your first lesson. I believe it gives his students a better understanding of him if they don't know," Ryan said. "It's also why I told you that you didn't have to worry about him saying anything. Riddick is a mute. I don't know if he can't speak or if he just chooses not to, but no one aboard the ship has ever heard him utter a single word. But, he is among the best trainers in all the Stellarnaut Armada."

Happy that she had someone to train her, Lena could only think about missing her session with Riddick for the next few days. "Ryan," she said as they stepped away from the trainer's list.

"Yeah," Ryan said as he fiddled with a display screen on the left arm of his suit.

"Captain Zephyr said I could join them when they go planetside tomorrow. If that's the case, I'll miss my training sessions with Riddick while I'm gone."

"That is a fact," Arcturus chimed in. "They believe the landing party will be off the ship for one week."

"That's at least seven sessions I'll miss," Lena complained. "I'm going to lose Riddick as my trainer, aren't I?"

"Not necessarily," Ryan said. "We probably should have waited until your return to book a trainer, but since we already did, I'm sure it will be fine."

Lena made a sideways glance at Ryan and said, "I don't think you really know if it'll be okay or not."

"I'm not sure, but if I had known you planned on going planetside, I wouldn't have initiated the introduction."

"Well, there's nothing we can do about it now," Lena said. "I'm not missing out on exploring another planet; I've dreamed of it my whole life."

"You may still be able to make your first couple of training sessions," Ryan said. "It seems the descent to Navaria has been delayed for a day because of technical difficulties. I have to go; Z needs my assistance in dealing with the issue."

"Is there anything we can help with?" Lena asked.

"Not now, but if something comes up, I'll let you know," Ryan said over his shoulder as he walked away.

Lena and Arcturus turned to leave the training room. She didn't feel as bad now that she knew she would get a few lessons in before they made the trip down. She decided she would tell Riddick about the trip down; surely, he'd understand. She was actually glad things got delayed; it could make a massive difference in her survival, having some training under her belt.

As they turned a corner and for the first time she noticed there weren't any other people around, Lena looked up at Arcturus and asked, "Why are you so protective of me, and what did you mean when you said I had to fulfill my destiny?"

Without missing a step and not looking down at her, Arcturus said, "I believe you are destined to save my people and, in turn, the galaxy."

Lena stopped in her tracks and stared at the back of his head. "What do you mean, you believe I'm destined to save your people and the galaxy?" she asked. "That's a lot to put on me, isn't it?"

"Lena," Arcturus stopped and turned to look at her. "My people have gone into hiding. We have been doing so for many thousands of years. This is due to us being hunted for our life force."

"Hold on," Lena interrupted him. "What are you talking about? Your life force, what does that mean?"

"I would rather we not be in the open when I tell you what you must know," Arcturus said. "Could we go to your private chambers so we may discuss this matter privately?"

Lena sighed but turned and led the way to her room. Her mind was racing, *"What is he going on about? How do his people have anything to do with me? I just want to hunt down the people who killed my family."* They arrived at her room before she even realized she was walking in the correct direction.

She pushed some buttons on the door, and the lock clicked, allowing her access to the room. Once inside, she walked to the other side of the room and started removing the armor from her suit. As she was doing so, she looked at Arcturus and said, "Go on."

Arcturus took a deep breath, one that was unnecessary because of his anatomy; he didn't need to breathe like humans do. It was more of himself imitating human behavior. He had spent the last twenty-five years among beings of people, and their mannerisms were wearing on him.

"Let me start by properly introducing myself to you, Lena Zoravic. My name is Arcturus Steelborne. I am a member of the Biotan species from the planet Eldridia. We were a peaceful race before our home was invaded and our people were taken from their homes. We tried to fight back, but our enemies were relentless, and we were overpowered and defeated."

"Arcturus, you don't have to give me a full backstory, and that is incredible," Lena said. "I am sorry for what your people have gone through, but I don't understand where I come into all this."

"I am sorry, Lena," Arcturus seemed sad, more so than his normal upbeat self.

"Arcturus," Lena said, her tone soft as she walked over to him. "Come sit down and let's talk. I didn't mean to upset you."

"You did not upset me," he said. "It has been so long since I have been around my own people; just thinking of them existing in slavery upsets me greatly."

Lena took his hand in hers and looked into his eyes, and as sincerely as possible, she asked, "What do we need to do to free your people?"

Arcturus looked back at her, and just as seriously, he said, "I do not know."

"Hmm," Lena said. "Well, could you finish your story, and then we'll go from there?"

Arcturus nodded and got back to his feet. "After my people were taken hostage, my masters Xylar, Cygnus, and I each gathered a small group of our people. We loaded them into cryo ships and fled our home world. It has always been said that our people would leave Eldridia in need of rescue. It has also been said a Biotan technomancer would be responsible for guiding this rescue. Xylar or Cygnus were always thought to be the ones to lead the charge, not me."

"Technomancer?" Lena questioned the term.

"Technomancy is the magic of my people," Arcturus stated proudly. "I am a technomancer, and I believe my power was transferred to you when you awakened me."

"Wait, what?" Lena asked. "You believe what? Can you be more clear, please?"

"I believe my power has transferred to you," Arcturus said again. "I have been unable to tap fully into my power. I never was a powerful technomancer; however, my power was substantially greater before you."

"Maybe it's just because you just woke up, and your power hasn't fully returned," Lena suggested. She couldn't believe what he thought. How could she be a technomancer? What does that even mean?

"Lena, I know for you it seems like we just met a few days ago," Arcturus said. He sighed again as though he were about to hit her with some information. "I, however, have been awake for twenty-five years. If timing were my issue, I would have hoped it would have resolved itself by now."

"That would make sense," she said. "I keep forgetting about that."

Lena pulled the revolver from its holster in her leg armor and laid it on a shelf before she got back to her feet to remove the remaining armor from her suit. "Okay, let me get this straight." She removed the remaining armor and sat in a chair on the other side of the room. Pulling her legs up, she sat with her legs crossed in the chair. "You believe I am the savior of your people, and you also believe I have your tech-no-mancer," she spaced the word out as though she were saying it incorrectly, "powers?"

"Yes," Arcturus said without hesitation. "I believed it to be possible when you woke me up and told me you were hit with all the power that surged through the room. Then later, I was sure of it when you pulled upon my life force to electrocute Captain Blackwood after he killed your family."

Lena just looked at him, recalling the events he was talking about. She did get hit with a large surge, and she hadn't even remembered doing it until this moment, but she did do something that hurt Blackwood. "How had I forgotten that?" she asked herself. Then her mind went back to what he'd said about pulling on his life force. "What do you mean I pulled on your life force?" she asked him, wanting verification she heard him right.

"Technomancy is a magic that is possible due to the energy inside me," Arcturus said. "You have the ability to use that energy, but you lack the life force of a Biotan to use it. Therefore, for my people to be saved, we must work together. I need you for the power you possess, and you need me for the life force I possess."

Lena put her face in her hands and started rubbing her hands up and down her face, running her fingers into her hair as her hands went up her face. Through her covered face, she said, "This is all too much right now. Could we touch more on this later? I need to think about all this."

"Of course," Arcturus responded. "I will leave you to rest." He turned and headed to the door.

"Don't go," she said. "I want you to stay for a while before I go to sleep. I just don't want to be alone with my thoughts."

He stopped and looked back over his shoulder. "Very well." He turned back and went to the chair Lena was sitting in. He helped her to her feet, and then she went to her bed. He sat and looked at her for a long moment, then started scanning the room. Lena smiled at him and closed her eyes. She didn't know why, but she loved this strange person she dug up.

The next morning, Lena and Arcturus got up early and went to see Riddick Shaw for her first scheduled training session. During the walkover, Lena asked Arcturus, "Could you tell me how the technomancy works after my training session?"

Arcturus seemed about to hesitate at her request, obviously not expecting it from Lena so soon. "Yes, it would please me very much to do so," he responded, a small smile touching his lips for a brief second. Lena would have missed it had she not been looking right at him because it vanished just as fast as it appeared.

The next couple of hours were brutal for Lena. Riddick had been easy on her during their analysis session the day before. However, this morning's training consisted of Lena getting beaten up by Riddick because she didn't understand what he wanted her to do most of the time. "What do you want me to do?" she asked him at one moment while lying flat on her back. He stood over her, shaking his head. *"If he keeps beating me so badly, I won't be able to concentrate on anything Arcturus tries to tell me about technomancy later."*

Riddick stepped back and motioned for her to get up. Once she was on her feet, he instructed her to assume her stance. Once in position, he nodded his head back. This was a gesture she had come to know, which meant he wanted her to attack him. She did, and once again, she was punished for her mistakes. Lying on her back once again, she asked, "Can we take a break?"

Riddick tilted his head to the side, had an odd smirk on his face, and looked around the room as if insinuating something. His eyes stopped on Arcturus, and he shrugged his shoulders at him as if to convey something only they understood.

"What?" Lena asked, frustrated.

"I believe Riddick Shaw is trying to say there are no breaks in battle," Arcturus said.

Lena sighed and got to her feet. The next few attacks she initiated weren't as devastating as the prior ones. Sticking to it and learning from her previous mistakes, Lena was able to spar back and forth a little with Riddick by the end of practice. Once their time was up, Lena asked Riddick, "Why don't we wear the suits during training? Shouldn't I get used to wearing it while fighting?"

Riddick nodded, but then he hit Lena in the side. She doubled over in pain, and Riddick leaned over and picked her up. He placed his hand over where he had just struck her and squeezed slightly, then shook his hand. With his expression, he made it seem as though he were in pain and nodded his head. He walked over, picked up his suit, and held it out, shaking it. He then placed the suit against his body and mimicked hitting himself, followed by brushing the spot as if to indicate no pain.

"I see," Lena said. "With the suit, I won't feel the pain of the blow. Without knowing what the blow will do, why try to defend it, to begin with?" She stated her thoughts but said it as though she were questioning herself.

Riddick nodded and smiled. Lena couldn't help but smile back; it was the first time she'd seen the serious trainer smile.

"That makes sense," she said, then walked over to where Arcturus was sitting and observing the training session. "Are you ready to go?"

"Are you ready to go?" he asked in return. "The only reason I am here is due to your lack of combat training."

Lena shook her head and said, "You're hopeless." They walked from the training room and started back to her room. "I need to get my suit on. I am hurting so badly."

"That is an excellent idea," Arcturus said. "When you are done with your healing, we can discuss the technomancy and how it applies to you and the Biotan life force."

# Chapter 9

Ascendant 4

6552 ASST

Arcturus was giving Lena a brief history of his people and their god. "Technomancy is a magic that dates back to when the Biotans were first created by the god known as Chronotek. Lord Chrono, as we Biotans like to call him, created us in the image that he imagined the future to hold."

"Every Biotan is created with a piece of Chronotek inside them. This is the life force I speak of." He touched his chest, where the faint glow of white energy illuminated.

Lena looked down at her own chest and placed her hand against it. Knowing she didn't have a piece of a god there, she did know that's where her life force would be considered to come from. "I wish I had an unlimited life force from a god," she said.

"My life and every Biotan's life was created for one purpose. No matter how long our lives are, no matter what we learn, we have one reason for living. Lord Chrono has foreseen the devastating future this galaxy holds if it is not altered. The life force inside me is not mine; it's his. However, your life force is yours. You should cherish that, Lena Zoravic, for my life is not my own; it belongs to Chronotek."

Lena was shocked by this revelation. Arcturus, someone who seemed so free-spirited, was being held down by his history and his god's words. How could a god expect an entire race of people to live just to sustain a future that hadn't even come full circle?

"Arcturus, I hate that for you and your people," Lena said. "But if every Biotan was created to preserve or fix the future, we need to find them right now, don't we?"

"It is pertinent that the Biotans are located and freed," Arcturus stated. "However, we are currently under the command of one Captain, Janis Zephyr. We must obtain his trust, and he must gain our loyalty. It is only then that we will be able to convince him and his people to help us."

"Okay, if we still have time before everything comes around," Lena said. "We should probably get to how this technomancy magic works. How do I use it, and furthermore, how do I use your life force to power it?"

"Certainly," Arcturus said. "We will start with you pulling upon my life force. This will grant you the power to use technomancy."

Lena looked at him, puzzled. "How do I do that?" she asked.

Arcturus returned the puzzled look. "I do not know. I had the belief you knew how to do it. You have drawn power from me before."

"I know, you said that, but I don't remember what I did or what happened," Lena said. "It must have just been instinct when Blackwood shot Kian." Her voice broke a bit at the mention of his name.

"Maybe you can use the memory of Kian and your family as a conduit to siphon the power from me," Arcturus suggested.

Lena closed her eyes and thought about when Kian was

born and how happy she was to have a little brother. She was ten years old, and her father sat Kian in her lap so she could hold him. It was the happiest day of her life. She had always wanted to have a little sister, but Kian was perfect.

She opened her eyes, and she could see that Arcturus's chest was glowing a little brighter than before. Her body felt different, too; she could feel a pulsing deep inside her. The pulse wasn't unlike what she had felt when she had sensed the Zephyr suit pulsing through her body. No, it was more of an overwhelming feeling of energy, of life; it made her feel as though she could do anything.

"Now," Arcturus said, "You have my life force inside you. With the force you now control, you can enhance the technology around you."

Lena turned to the viewing monitor on the wall and thought about it being on, and it came on. Mentally, she shut it back off and then scanned the room. She eyed the Zephyr suit lying on the shelf and tried to activate the technology within it. The Zephyr suit was the most technological thing she'd ever seen, but she couldn't do anything with it. The power was still pulsing through her veins, so she knew she wasn't exhausted.

Looking back at Arcturus, she said, "I can't do anything with the suit. Isn't it a technology?"

"It is," Arcturus responded, "I have also tried to alter the suit's functions with what little power I have left. I have had no luck in doing so myself."

"Not thinking any more on it, other than the fact that Maximilian Zephyr's technology is tamper-proof," Lena turned her attention to the electronic doorway to leave her room. With a thought of the passcode, the door opened. "Could I have opened this door without knowing the passcode?" she asked Arcturus.

"I am unaware of the functionality of the security system in this ship," Arcturus said. "My abilities are limited; therefore, I have been unsuccessful in getting my mind into many devices on this vessel."

*I'll try another door at a later time,* she thought. She mentally shut the door to her room and started scanning for something else to mess with, but she could feel the overwhelming pulsing starting to diminish. With the last bit of energy she had left, she flipped the room lights out. Her next thought was to turn them back on, but she couldn't. The energy was gone. Reaching her hands out in front of her, she started fumbling to the other side of the darkroom to flip the switch to bring the lights back on. Once the lights were on, she looked at Arcturus and said, "That was actually pretty cool. We will definitely need to work on learning more about that later. For now, though, I think we need to get some food and then some rest. Tomorrow is a big day."

After a good meal and a decent night's sleep, Lena went back to the training room. Before her training session started, she said, "Riddick, I need you to know something. I don't want to lose you as a trainer, but today, I leave for a week. Captain Zephyr invited me to go planetside when they go to Navaria." A strange look was all she got in return.

Riddick had a unique training session set up for her this morning. There was no combat training, no weapons training, no strength training. Instead, they just sat on the floor, legs crossed, hands on their knees. *Why am I just sitting here? This is stupid,* she thought.

She looked up at Riddick, his eyes closed, and his hands turned palm up in his lap. Shaking her head, she took a deep breath, closed her eyes, and placed her hands on her lap palm up. Taking the moment of quiet and the time she had, she started thinking about her mom and the way she felt when her mom turned to her and smiled, holding Kian for the first time. Lena was proud to be the sister of the little boy her mother had just given birth to hours before.

"Hello, my child," a strange voice said."

Lena's thoughts left that hospital room, and her eyes popped open. But when they did, she wasn't sitting in the training room anymore. Instead, she was nowhere. There was nothing around her; it was just an open space with a haze all around.

Then the voice came again. "Lena Zoravic."

She looked around, and she could see the outline of someone, but she couldn't make out who.

"You are stronger than you know, my child," the voice said again. Lena opened her eyes once more, breathing heavily. She looked around; Arcturus was sitting on a bench, scanning the room. Unsure of what had just happened, she turned her gaze to Riddick. He was looking at her in a way she hadn't seen before, nodding his head before standing to his feet. Lena watched as he walked over to the schedule board on the wall and made some marks.

Once he walked away, Lena, still breathing hard, approached the board to see what he had written down. All her training sessions for the next week were marked out, and he had penciled in additional sessions for the days following. *He must know I'm going planetside with Captain Zephyr*, she thought.

"Well, that's a good thing," she said to Arcturus, who had walked up beside her as she scanned the schedule. "Now I don't have to worry about losing him as my trainer."

"I, too, have come to the same conclusion," Arcturus responded. "Ryan Patel was correct in his assumption of 'it should be fine,'" Arcturus tried to imitate the young Stellarnaut.

Lena laughed out loud at his attempt at mockery. "Tha... Tha..." She held up her hand as she tried to get her laughter under control. While inhaling a deep breath, her mind began to clear the form she'd encountered during her meditation. She let it out slowly to control her laughter. Once she regained control, she said, "That was great, Arcturus. I probably wouldn't do that around Ryan, but you can do it around me all you want."

They left the training room and headed to the hangar. Lena couldn't help but start thinking about what had happened during training. *What was that about?"* she thought. *I'll talk to Arcturus about it once we return from Navaria.*

They stepped through the door to the hangar, the very one she first landed in when they came aboard Ascendant 4. Once inside the hangar, while standing on the upper deck, it was easy to spot Captain Zephyr and his sidekick, Emily Chen. The black Zephyr suit stood out like a Stinger-class fighter ship would if it were in a hangar full of Phoenix-class ships.

"Lena and Arcturus made their way over to the captain and Chen, despite the fact that Lena couldn't care less about seeing or being around Chen ever again.

"Ah, Lena, Arcturus," Captain Zephyr greeted them as they walked up. "I assume your training session went well this morning?"

"Yes, thank you," Lena responded. "It was a very strange training session, but it was good." She didn't want to say too much about what had happened.

"Strange?" Zephyr said. "Yeah, you'll have that with Shaw. I can't complain about his results, but his methods are definitely strange compared to my other trainers."

"I, too, find Riddick Shaw to be a strange human," Arcturus added."

Captain Zephyr looked at Arcturus and nodded. "We're still waiting for Patel and Z; once they're here, we'll head out. In the meantime, let me introduce you to the rest of my landing team."

He turned and walked around the other side of the Phoenix. They were all congregating around, and they came to see two individuals standing there.

"Rodriguez," Captain Zephyr shouted. "I don't mind members of my crew dating. We all live together for years on end; I get it. But if I have to tell you to keep your hands to yourself while on duty one more time, I'll have you back in the weapon room cleaning weapons instead of firing them."

A young man with dark hair and light tan skin smiled and said, holding his hands out in front of himself and pumping them back and forth, "Woo woo woo, Cap, calm down with that cleaning detail. You know Ava is just so damn irresistible. But I will keep your request in mind."

Rodriguez winked at the captain, who just smiled. "And who do we have here?" He said, looking at Lena. "She's pretty and all, but if you're trying to bait me into steering clear of Ava, it ain't going to work."

The girl whom Rodriguez was just caressing slapped him on the back of the head. "I don't care how pretty she is, Max. Don't be saying it in front of me."

"If you two are done," Zephyr said, "I would like to introduce you to two new members of the team. Well, they're accompanying us on the trip down to Navaria." The captain stepped over to the young man he was just scolding and said, "This is Max Rodriguez. He is our heavy weapons specialist. This boy can improvise a weapon out of some of the most useless materials you can imagine. And to his right..." Zephyr stepped over beside the young lady and continued, "Ava Ramirez. She is the best pilot we've seen since your dad left us."

"Her dad?" Ava asked. Then recognition kicked in, and she said, "Darian Zoravic? You're Darian's kid?"

"Yes, Ramirez," Captain Zephyr said. "I would like to introduce Lena Zoravic, and our Biotan friend here is Arcturus." He turned his attention to Lena and added, "Ramirez was your dad's co-pilot back in the day. He taught her everything she knows."

"Well," she chimed in, "He taught me everything I knew up to the time he left. How's your old man doing these days? I'd like to see him again; he was one of my favorite people when he was here."

"Darian Zoravic was shot down and killed twenty-five years ago," Captain Zephyr said, trying to keep Lena from having to answer the question. "We picked Lena up on Zorath shortly after it happened. Darian enacted the Stellarnaut protection protocol, and she's been in cryosleep until a few weeks ago. She and Arcturus here are going to join us, and we're not going to hound her about her father."

Both Ramirez and Rodriguez nodded. Just then, Emily, who had been poking at her ArmComm, spoke up, saying, "The rogue Stellarnaut has just been spotted again. He's nearing Voltain, and I still bet he's heading to Sol. I'm not sure why; it just seems that if a Stellarnaut goes rogue, they'd be after the leader."

"We'll worry about that once we're back from Navaria," the captain said. He turned to Ava and said, "Let's get this bird fired up; Z and Patel just walked in."

Navaria 6552 ASST

Lena settled herself into a seat in the passenger bay at the back of the Phoenix. She didn't know much about this class of ship; it wasn't listed in any of the spacecraft or fighter ship books she owned. There were far more passenger seats than she remembered from her first ride. Ryan and Z made their way up the ramp at the back of the ship.

Ryan stowed his bag in a cargo hold above the seat and sat adjacent to Lena's seat. Arcturus was seated to Lena's right and Ryan to her left. Z walked over and sat in the seat across from Lena. He sat there, staring at her; his white, glowing eye freaked her out; she hoped he wouldn't say anything. His voice scared her more than his appearance did.

As though he were reading her mind, he said, in his static-filled voice, "Lena Zoravic, how did you manage to convince Captain Zephyr not only to get you a suit but also to allow you to join us on this trip planet-side? Do not mind me asking. I am just curious to know."

Lena looked to Ryan for help in answering the question. Ryan was facing the front of the ship, talking with Max about a device Max wanted Ryan to make to add to one of his weapons.

She turned back to Z and said, "It was my father's old suit. I know it's not as modern as everyone else's, but I like it."

"I see. I had noticed it was a second-generation Zephyr suit," Z responded, the static in his voice causing Lena to cringe. She attempted to hide it, but the look on Z's face told her she failed in her attempt. "But you didn't tell me how you convinced him to allow you to join us."

Lena swallowed and cleared her throat. "I have information about the Navarians, and Captain Zephyr needed that knowledge for himself. I've always wanted to explore other planets." She was so terrified talking to this man that her voice broke slightly as she spoke. Attempting to conceal her fear, she continued, "So, I made a deal with him. I would allow him access to my books, and in return, he would allow me to explore Navaria."

Z just nodded and started to speak again when Ryan's voice came from her left. "Z's not scaring you? Is he?" he asked. "I know he's kinda scary looking, no offense, Z," Ryan said, glancing up at the masked man. He turned his attention back to Lena. "But he's not all that bad of a guy."

Lena turned to Ryan, relief evident on her face. "No, he just had a few questions, that's all."

Just then, the ship lifted off its landing pad, and the hangar door opened, giving them access to the outside of the ship. Lena strained her neck as they approached the opening, trying to see outside the ship. She wanted to see what Navaria looked like from as far out as possible, to take in the planet's beauty.

Navaria came into view as the Phoenix left the bay door. She had seen Zorath from the reaches of space only once on the day she left, but Navaria was absolutely beautiful compared to

Zorath's dull red. She didn't believe Zorath to be an ugly planet; it was her home, after all. But Navaria was something to behold, with green and blue swirls all about the planet and white clouds breaking up the greens and blues.

As they moved closer, it became clearer that the blues she was seeing were seas the planet had to offer, something that was a rare commodity on Zorath. They would typically have water shipped in and put in a holding tank at her home. The greens were the vegetation of the planet, another rarity on Zorath. Lena couldn't believe how many trees and plants were on the surface of this planet; it was unlike anything she had ever seen before.

"We've just got the go-ahead for landing, Captain," Ava said from the pilot's seat. "I'm taking us down. Max, prepare yourself for any hostile encounters. Everyone, keep your eyes peeled. Watch out for any sudden movements."

"Stand down for now, Rodriguez," Captain Zephyr said. "We're here to help at the request of these people, and everything we've learned about them says they're not hostile unless provoked. With that in mind, stay on guard but do not unnecessarily provoke the locals. Let's not create more problems for ourselves than we already face."

Max, who had already started heading to the back hatch with his large plasma blaster, stopped and returned to his seat. He did not, however, relinquish his weapon. It stood linked to a cable that ran to an armored pack on his back. Once the firearm was hooked to the cable, it hummed to life, and the white glow illuminated through the coils in the weapon.

Max looked at Lena and said, hoisting his gun up a bit, "This bad boy could blast a hole the size of your head through the heart of any enemy ship, vehicle, or structure. If stuff goes south, just stick with me, and you'll be fine." He winked and turned his attention back to Captain Zephyr. The young Stellarnaut also had two laser pistols, one at each of his hips.

Arcturus, who had been listening intently to what Max was saying, spoke up, "Due to the size of his weapon and the amount of energy harnessed in his pack, I believe Max Rodriguez's claim to be true." He, too, turned his attention to Captain Zephyr, who was briefing them on their mission and how they planned to execute it.

"We have permission to enter Navaria's atmosphere," Zephyr said when Lena turned her attention to him. "And as far as we know, our host is a friendly species. They sent out a distress call a few weeks ago. As with any other deployment, this could be a ploy to get us planet-side where we can be overrun. I highly doubt that is the case with everything I've read about the Navarians, but we can never be too cautious."

"So, we're not here to kick the Navarians' asses?" Max asked.

"No, Rodriguez," Captain Zephyr said firmly. "If anything, I'd say we're here to help. There could be danger, though, and that's why you are here. If there is trouble, I'll need you to put that new weapon of yours to the test." He looked at each one of them. "We're meant to meet with the ruling members of their society. I expect each of you to be on your best behavior while maintaining a sense of seriousness and keeping a watchful eye out for anything out of the ordinary."

Everyone nodded as they looked around the Phoenix cabin. "Loud and clear, Cap," Ava said from the cockpit. With that, she descended the spacecraft down to the surface of Navaria and landed it flawlessly on their designated landing pad.

Each group made their way from the ship down the loading ramp at the rear. As it lowered, Lena could start to see the surface of another planet for the first time. It was beautiful; there were trees as far as she could see. The Navarian city was built in the middle of a huge forest.

As they walked down the ramp, Lena could see other aircraft on other landing pads. These were for the on-planet flight, which was all Lena could figure, considering the Navarians never left their planet, according to the information in her books.

The housing was attached to the side of trees, which were remarkably large, much larger than anything Lena had ever seen back home. For people who lived in trees, their technology was up to date with Zorath, if not more advanced. Many overhead walkways allowed the Navarians to travel from tree to tree to the platforms and other housing facilities. They were currently following two Navarians who had spoken to Captain Zephyr when he departed the Phoenix.

The Navarians were tall, slender people with long, pointed ears. Their skin tone ranged from a light pastel green to a light pastel blue, which was true for the two they were following at the moment. The clothing they wore wasn't much different from Lena's everyday attire. *These beings aren't that much different than us,* Lena thought as she observed her surroundings.

They were led into a large building constructed in a ground-level clearing. From what Lena could tell, it seemed like their housing was in the trees, but their markets and other everyday-use buildings were at ground level. The buildings looked like the ones she had seen in photos in her book. A major difference in these buildings was that most of the buildings she'd seen were squared; this building was round like most others here.

The two lead Navarians opened a big double door, each of them opening one. They stepped to the side, allowing the group to enter.

"Rodriguez, Ramirez, wait out here," Captain Zephyr said. "I would prefer we're not all confined inside this structure should things go south."

Max and Ava each stepped to the side, standing next to the two Navarians holding the doors open. The Navarian near Max instructed the two remaining team members to enter the building.

"I think we'll stay right here, Ears," Max said. "Captain's orders."

The Navarian standing near Ava gestured for her to enter the building. She, too, denied the request to enter the building. Without another word being said, the Navarian's eyes glowed, each glowing the same color as the skin. Then Max and Ava were slowly and gently ushered into the building by a force at their backs. Lena swallowed deeply and thought, *Whelp, looks like we're going to be captured after all. We should have never come here with so few soldiers.*

"What in the heck was that?" Max asked. "Y'all got some sort of magic powers to force people to move when they don't want to?"

"It's telekinesis," Lena said. "Telekinesis is also something the book says about the Navarians."

"Exactly," Captain Zephyr said. "I was hoping they would demonstrate it to us if I were to separate our group. Another point mentioned in your book is that they don't care about their visitors posting sentries in their cities. I had to try it."

"How'd you know they wouldn't try to kill us?" Max asked.

Zephyr just looked at Max with a look of disappointment and shook his head. "You're a Stellarnaut, Rodriguez. You and I could more than likely defeat this entire city without the assistance of the rest of our party, even with their telekinetic powers."

"That's right!" Max said, all his confidence back. The statement from Captain Zephyr also made Lena feel better about the situation and not being captured.

The interior of the building had a modern look. The walls were decorated with photos of who seemed to be past leaders or members of their council here. In the back of the room was a table that was constructed at the same curvature in the outer wall of the building. Behind the table sat five elderly-looking Navarians.

The one who sat in the center of the table stood and said, in a similar monotone voice as the younger Navarian who'd spoken earlier, "Greetings, friend Stellarnauts."

Captain Zephyr inclined his head and said, "Thank you for the invitation into your beautiful city. How could we be of service to you all today? Getting right to business."

"Very well," he said. "Let me first start by introducing each member of our council." He turned and pointed to the far left of the table. "At the far end is my sister, Thalara; next to her is Arannis."

Turning right and starting from the furthest point again, he said, "At this end, we have Elara, and next to her is Solarius. Each of them rules over areas of Navaira: to the north he pointed to his sister, east pointing to Arannis, south he gestured to Elara, and to the west he laid his hand on Solarius's shoulder." He then pointed to himself and said, "I am Lyraeth, ruler of central Navaria and mediator over each other area."

"So, you're the king, and they each oversee your land?" Max asked.

"Rodriguez," Captain Zephyr said through clenched teeth. "Keep your mouth shut until spoken to."

"Sorry, Cap'," Max said. Lena was beginning to realize that Max Rodriguez couldn't keep his mouth shut regardless of the situation.

"To answer your question, Rodriguez? Did I pronounce that correctly? Please tell me otherwise." Lyraeth asked.

Max just nodded his head, even though it was apparent he wanted to say something about how the "R" didn't roll with the monotone sound coming from the Navarian's voice.

"Yes, in your old-world functionality, I would be considered the king, and these four would rule under me in other lands," Lyraeth answered. "Back to the problem at hand, the reason we asked you here. Our planet has unfortunately been invaded by an outside species, and we would like for you all to look into this for us. We shall be extremely grateful if you can help us out because we have no one to turn to"

"Don't y'all have an army…" Max cut himself off before he could finish due to the look he received from Zephyr, Ava,

Ryan, and Z. He held his hands out in front of himself, palms open, "Sorry."

Captain Zephyr turned his attention back to Lyraeth and asked, "Do you know the location or a close whereabouts of the invading aliens?"

"To the south, just before the forest ends, before you enter swamp lands," Lyraeth answered. "I've arranged for you to have a guide to show you around." He turned and said, "Bring me Lyra Nova."

Two younger Navarians brought forth a young female who looked to be of Navarian origin, but her skin tone was very light green, and her ears were nowhere near as pointed as those of the other Navarians they'd seen here. She was about a foot shorter than the other Navarians, too.

"Who is this?" Captain Zephyr asked.

"Lyra Nova," Lyraeth answered. "She will guide you to the location of the invading species. She is very well versed in the lands outside the city limits. You will not have any problem getting around with her guiding you."

The two Navarians led Lyra over to the Stellarnaut party, then bowed and backed away.

Lyra glared at each of them and came to Captain Zephyr, saying, "You must be the leader of this group. Come on, the sooner we get this done, the sooner I can get back to my peaceful life." The look on her face when she said the words displayed disgust. This gave Lena the impression that the young Navarian woman did not live a very peaceful life.

She walked right between the group of Stellarnauts and

headed for the door. Each of them looked to Zephyr, who shrugged his shoulders and started to follow the young Navarian. Each of them, in turn, followed their captain's lead.

# Chapter 11

Navaria

6552 ASST

When they walked out of the town, Emily's ArmComm beeped. She poked it a few times with her pen. Her eyes scanned back and forth a few moments before they opened wide with surprise. She brought Captain Zephyr's attention to the device so he could see what was displayed on the screen. After reading what was displayed, the captain looked over his shoulder at the group of soldiers following him. He turned back, leaned over, and whispered into Emily's ear.

Lena couldn't make out exactly what he was saying, but what she did hear sounded something along the lines of, "We'll discuss this after we're finished with this mission." Not wanting to pry, she didn't even bring it to anyone else's attention. However, she would ask the captain as soon as she got a chance. Her curiosity had increased tenfold, but she focused on the mission ahead, knowing it was a priority.

Lyra Nova proved to be an excellent guide when it came to navigating the wilderness of the Navaria forest they were trudging through. The foliage was dense, filled with thick hanging vines and branches. The wildlife here was unlike anything Lena had ever seen or read about. There were reptilian-type creatures that had six legs and two tails. They were more than three times the size of the largest lizard on Zorath and could climb in the trees and jump from limb to limb with extreme accuracy and agility. The feline-type mammals were even more agile than the reptiles. However, they had only four legs like most cats on Zorath but no tail and could move through the forest without making a sound. Lyra had to point out these creatures to them. They seemed harmless, and the crew did not disturb them as they did not want to cause any unnecessary attention to themselves.

"You must keep your eyes open and alert, Captain Zephyr, while in the jungles of Navaria," Lyra said. She stopped and knelt behind a tree and pointed out one of the cats. "Watch very closely; it is tracking smaller prey. Looking to feed its fam…"

Just then, a loud screech came from behind them, causing each of them to jump and turn in that direction. All but Lyra, who was still watching the feline. The cat turned and saw the group with their backs facing it, and it turned and lunged in their direction. It looked at the team as its enemy and did not hesitate to attack them. This was totally unexpected.

Lena turned when she heard a thudding sound coming from behind. When she saw the large cat running at her, her instincts kicked in, and she started pulling energy from Arcturus. It was an incredible sight to behold!

"Why in the Sam hell is your robot glowing?" Max asked while looking at Arcturus. "He ain't going to blow up, is he?"

"I am not. Just wait and watch," Arcturus assured him.

Lena, now full of the Biotan's energy, stretched her arm out to strike the thing down just as she had done to Blackwood. "Cat!" Lena yelled, pointing at the coming feline.

The team was ready to defend themselves. Max turned and raised his weapon, pointing it at the approaching animal. He opened fire with the ether-lumina-powered plasma blaster. The weapon put out more blasts of energy than Lena would have imagined; it was stunning. White bolts of energy denigrated that cat, not to mention what it did to the surrounding trees. Max's reaction allowed Lena to relinquish the pull she had on Arcturus. She almost gave her secret away. It was an excellent show of teamwork, and Lena was the star.

"Why did you do that?" Lyra screamed at Max. "You do realize now that every predator in the area knows we're here now. Not to mention, I could have taken care of it without having to end its life."

"I ain't sure if you noticed or not," Max said. "But that thing was about to attack my group. I am charged with the protection of this party, and that's what I'm going to do exactly. I cannot at any point sabotage the safety and security of the party." He pointed to the spot where the cat used to exist. "If you don't intend for them to die, don't allow them to get that close to my friends. If I had not made a move, we would have been minced meat by now."

"Come on," Zephyr said. "We need to get out of here. Lyra, could you get us clear of this area and back on track? We have a better time during this skirmish. "

Lyra nodded, and they moved through the destroyed area of the forest. They were well beyond its location before any other animals made their way there.

Once they were clear and things had slowed down, Lena approached Lyra, who was leading the group. "I hope you do not mind me asking, but you seem rather different than the other Navarians here," Lena said.

Lyra turned and looked at the young girl and said, "Yeah, so."

"No, please don't take my thoughts or what I'm asking wrong," Lena said. "I'm just curious as to why. I'm just nervous, but at the same time, my curious nature wouldn't let me go much longer without asking, so I just had to ask."

"It's a touchy subject; I prefer not to talk about it. Thank you," Lyra said.

Lena just nodded and kept pace with the young Navarian, making it as though she were helping keep a watchful eye out. In reality, she had no clue what she was looking for or watching out for other than large cats.

"What are you doing?" Lyra asked.

"Keeping a lookout for any other dangers," Lena responded.

"Yeah, but why are you doing it next to me?" Lyra asked.

"The guys back there are all talking about Max's gun and how much damage it did to that car and the forest," Lena said. "I'm not really interested in Max's gun, and Ava doesn't really talk, nor does it seem like she wants me around. Plus, I'm more interested in you and your people right now. I've always been fascinated with exploring and learning about what is out in the galaxy."

"Well, you've definitely stumbled upon one of the most unique things in all of the galaxy," Lyra said.

"Oh yeah?" Lena asked. "And what's that?"

Lyra looked over her shoulder to see if any of the other members of the group were in earshot. "The reason I look different is because I am different." She looked over her shoulder again before she asked, "Can you keep a secret?"

"Yeah," Lena leaned in close, showing so much interest in knowing a secret. She couldn't believe this girl was going to tell her something about herself.

"Well, I don't believe you," Lyra said. "You have to tell me something about yourself first, something meaningful. Not just your favorite food or anything."

Lena thought about that for a moment, *Should I tell her about my technomancy power?* Deciding against that, she pulled the revolver from her side and said, "My family was killed with this," she said, showing Lyra the gun. "I haven't told anyone yet, but I plan on tracking down the person who killed them and using the same weapon he used to end his life."

"Slow down there, killer," Lyra said. "Put that thing away. I commend you for your ambition for revenge." Lyra looked over her shoulder again, noticing the rest of the group was still far enough back to where they could still talk in private. "The reason I'm different from other Navarians is that I'm only half Navarian."

"What?" Lena asked. "How is that possible?"

"Like I said before, I'm a unique find for you on your explorations," Lyra said. She took a deep breath and said, "Several years ago, some people came here before I was born. They were human soldiers of the Intergalactic Star Fleet. From my understanding, they were here to do research on my people; they were very interested in our telekinetic abilities."

"Telekinetic abilities," Lena said with excitement in her voice. *'If she has telekinesis, that would make talking to someone about my powers so much easier.'*

"Yeah," Lyra said. "Let me finish; this is hard enough as it is."

"I'm sorry."

Lyra continued, "Like I was saying, they were interested in our telekinetic powers; they would take some Navarians up to their mothership, or whatever they call it, to try to study them, but once a Navarian leaves the planet's surface, they become weak and cannot live. Our connection to the planet is strong and unforgiving. Apparently, the leader of the Star Fleet was hoping to be able to strip the Navarians of their powers for themselves. At least that's the story I heard before my mother passed away."

"So, your mother. Was…she…human or Navarian?" Lena asked.

"She was a Navarian," Lyra said, glancing over her shoulder before leaning in close to Lena and whispering, "She was raped by one of the soldiers. She never did tell me who he was before she died. The result of the rape was..." Lyra lifted her hands and gestured downward.

"So," Lena whispered back, leaning in, "You're half human and half Navarian?"

"Yes," Lyra replied with distaste in her voice. "You and I have something in common. I share the same vengeance plans as you, except I don't have a weapon to carry them out with. If I ever figure out a way to leave this place, I'm going to hunt my father down and kill him for the pain he put my mother through.

She died young because of the strain on her body from giving birth to me. It isn't natural for two species to mate and have offspring."

"Why don't you come with us? You would be an excellent addition to our team," Lena said.

"Can't. My ties to Navaria will kill me," Lyra explained.

"But...but... what about your human side? You can't neglect that!" Lena almost couldn't get the words out fast enough. "Do you think since you have human blood, you could survive off the planet?"

Lyra's eyes opened in recognition. "I've never considered the possibility of my human side allowing me to do so, but you're right. It could be possible for me to leave? I've never tried. I have to think about this, Lena. You know, now that you said all of this, it would be great to be with you all."

"You should come with us when we leave," Lena said, almost too optimistically.

"Your captain wouldn't let me tag along. I just know it," Lyra said, all her hope draining from her face.

"He let me come along after my family was killed, so don't worry about it. " Lena said

"I'm not really a Stellarnaut," Lena confessed. "I only have this suit because my dad was one, and this is his old suit from before he left the Armada. So I am a Stellarnaut thanks to this suit!"

"Yeah, I noticed your suit was of an older fashion but wasn't going to say anything. I kept wondering, but now that you have explained, it is pretty clear."

"We can talk to Captain Zephyr once we're done with this mission. You have my back, and you shall come with us," Lena proposed.

"Okay, looks like we're getting close to the edge of the forest," Lyra announced, turning her attention to the rest of the group. "We're approaching the outer perimeter of the forest. We'll be close to the invaders soon. Let's keep our eyes peeled."

Lyra motioned for Captain Zephyr to come closer. She pointed out to the edge of the forest. "Just beyond these trees, there's a clearing. We need to sneak to the outer perimeter, and then I can show you where the invaders are coming from. Get ready, everyone!"

Zephyr nodded. "Let's move. The sooner we infiltrate their base of operations, the sooner we can get back to the Ascendant 4. Time is of the essence!"

The group moved closer to the edge of the forest, Lena doing her best to conceal her nervousness. She crossed the last few feet of cover and stepped out into the opening of the field before her head was suddenly snapped forward as she was pulled back into the forest.

"What are you thinking?" Z said to her as she lay on the ground at his feet. "We are in hostile territory; you are not to step into danger like that. We must tread carefully.."

"Sorry, I didn't realize," She said, rubbing her neck. "You could have broken my neck, throwing me like that, I swear!"

"You'll be fine," Ryan said. "Your Zephyr suit will notice your discomfort soon and soothe your pain. You should be more mindful of your location and the seriousness of the situation." He then turned his attention back to the opening beyond the forest.

"There it is," Lyra said, pointing across the field. "There's a faint yellowish glowing structure out there. That's where they're coming and going from. Can you see?"

"Where exactly are they coming from?" Captain Zephyr asked. "That yellowish glow is some sort of teleporter. I wonder what it could be about."

Lyra looked up in the sky and pointed, "There's a transport ship in orbit. That's what I've been told, anyway, but it's anyone's guess what it could be."

Captain Zephyr observed his crew. "Emily, could you sneak up and get a closer look at the device? Let's try to find out what it is exactly."

The light-footed woman nodded. She punched a few buttons on her device, and her suit took on a chameleon look. Emily blended with her surroundings; she was noticeable, but Lena thought if she looked away, she would possibly lose the spy's location.

Everyone watched Emily as she tracked across the field, blending with the tall weeds. Her movement was flawless as she made her way along with the slight breeze that blew across the land. It was incredible how she blended with the surroundings and moved like a cheetah. Her skills proved very useful here.

Lena stepped closer to the captain and asked in a hushed voice, "What was it that Chen showed you on her device back when we first left the town?"

He glanced her way for a split second, then squatted down slightly. "It's nothing that concerns you; I wouldn't worry about it." Then he went back to watching Emily as she made her way across the field. Without looking back in her direction, he said,

"You must quit eavesdropping on other people's conversations."

*I wasn't thinking it had anything to do with me,* she sighed. *I just want to know what's going on. Plus, you all were talking right in front of me. I wasn't eavesdropping. Emily's face was very serious when she looked at her device. Something serious has had to have happened,* she thought.

Clearing her mind of concerns about what might be happening elsewhere, Lena focused on recalling where she had last seen Emily. Scanning the field, she couldn't find the sneaky woman. *The cloaking system on her suit is pretty good,* Lena thought. *I know she's there somewhere but can't find her. This is incredible and unbelievable! She is as swift as a fox!*

Captain Zephyr tapped Lena's shoulder, causing her to nearly jump out of her Zephyr suit.

Looking up at him, Lena saw he was pointing a few feet to the left of the yellow glowing device in the field. Once he did so, Lena spotted Emily's shimmering form once again. "Worry about what's going on here," Captain Zephyr whispered. "We'll concern ourselves with other matters once our mission is complete. Let's stay focused because we do not want to be taken by surprise like before."

Lena nodded, keeping an eye on Emily's movement. As much as she hated the woman for the way she'd been treated by her, Lena still didn't want anything bad to happen to her. She had already seen too much pain in her short life so far. Lena was someone who did not feel vengeful toward others because it would not help her cause. Having lost her family, she would not want anyone else to be hurt, even if they did not get along.

Footsteps sounded from behind, and then an unknown voice spoke up, "I hope Sivik gets the desired outcome with this group. I'm tired of chasing these aliens across the galaxy. I want to go home now. I have had enough!"

"Hey, you need to quit complaining about Emperor Sivik," another voice retorted. "If it wasn't for him, we wouldn't have the lives we have. We'd have been dead centuries ago. We owe everything to him, so please stop the whining."

"I know," the first voice conceded. "I just don't understand why he feels the need to possess all the powers of all alien species. This hunger for power could be his downfall, but why do we care anyway? It's not our concern. We have just hired guns, and he may even dispose of us after he does not need us anymore."

The second man stopped and said, "You do realize that you're talking about our Emperor? Don't you? If he's to lead this galaxy to become the galaxy we need, his authority must be followed. To do so, he has to be the most powerful being in the galaxy, and we are to be the most powerful fleet in all of the galaxy. If he wins, we win; therefore, it is a win-win situation for everyone. Please respect the Emperor because you know we owe our lives to him."

"Hmm," the first man scoffed. "What about the Stellarnauts? Those galaxy explorers?"

"I'm not worried about those Stellarnauts or whatever you call them," the second man said. "And neither should you. They think they're all mighty with their Zephyr suits, but their forces are minuscule compared to ours. We can take them down very easily. Our might against those suits, and you know who will win."

"How can you be so sure? Have you ever faced one?" the first man asked.

"No, but that's irrelevant to the fact that the Intergalactic Star Fleet is far superior to the Stellarnaut Armada. There is no contest at all whatsoever, so I do not need to face one to prove our superiority over those meddling explorers."

"You never know. They could be mercenaries."

"They could be whatever, but they can't take us on. Now get back to work, and enough complaining!"

Throughout the conversation between these two, Captain Zephyr motions for his soldiers to hold their positions. Lena hadn't taken her eyes off Emily, wanting to make sure the woman knew she would be having company. Lena pulled on Arcturus's life force ever so slightly, drawing just enough power to reach out with her mind and pull on the ArmComm on Emily's wrist. Their partnership was incredible and vital to the mission, and Lena had to be very careful when harnessing Arcturus's life force.

Emily, who was nearing the glow of the device, looked up just as the Star-Fleet soldiers walked by Lena. When they walked by, Lena glanced their way to try to get a look at them. She couldn't see their faces, but she did see they were wearing armored suits similar to the Zephyr suit but with a less sleek design. The armor was bulkier, even more so than the Zephyr suit she wore herself. There was a large protrusion coming out of the back. It looked like extra reinforcement to the spine. Their helmets were rounded with tubes coming out of the back and reaching down to the back just below the extra reinforcement. These guys were tough soldiers and would be more than a match for the Stellarnauts. It's like the irresistible force meeting the immovable object.

They were dragging an unknown species between them. The creature had a triangular-shaped head and limbs like those of an insect from Lena's home world of Zorath. It had an outer shell that was layered in orange, brown, and then white on the bottom side. Something seemed pretty off about that creature.

Therefore, not knowing what these creatures were, Lena scanned them with her suit's built-in OmniSight scanner:

Species: Xenolian Homeworld: Synthara

Type: Arthropod Ability: Telekinesis

After reading the description, she nudged Captain Zephyr and whispered, "I think Sivik is trying to obtain the power of telekinesis. There is no other reason he has sent his men here." She showed him the readout on her ArmComm screen.

The two Star-Fleet soldiers, along with the Xenolian, walked through the yellow-swirling light and vanished. Before stepping through the portal, Emily discreetly placed a tracker on the back of one of the soldier's armors.

The rest of the group hurried over to Emily's location to discuss what was going on with these Xenolians. Once everyone was together, Captain Zephyr spoke up, "Seems like we've gotten ourselves in the middle of one of Sivik's most recent scandals."

"Does your tracker show the location of the soldier now, Chen?" Z asked.

Looking at her ArmComm, Emily nodded, "Yes, they are currently in orbit of Navaria."

"What's the plan, Cap'?" Max inquired. "Are we going to invade that ship? Or continue looking for the rest of the invading species? Whatever we do, we have to make a decision now."

"Let's take it to a vote. Those in favor of tracking the rest of the Xenolians, raise your hand." Captain Zephyr surveyed the crew. Lena noticed only Arcturus had his hand up.

"Looks like the robot wants to let the Xenolian we just saw get cut up by Emperor Sivik's crazy wife," Max remarked.

"That is not what my intentions are for voting," Arcturus clarified. "I believe we will be outnumbered if we are to go to the Intergalactic Star-Fleet ship. It is in the best interest of everyone present that we take the path that leads to rescuing multiple Xenolians while keeping us safe and intact. I have suggested the path of least resistance, and we can preserve our security and safety."

"Where'd you find this bot, Cap'?" Max asked. "Obviously, the other Xenolians aren't going anywhere. Besides, it's our duty as Stellarnauts to intervene in any nefarious dealings that involve capturing alien species. We have to abide by our duty."

Captain Zephyr glared at Max. "He's only trying to look out for everyone's best interest, namely Lena's, I believe. Arcturus, we can't knowingly let the creature we just saw be taken aboard that ship to slaughter by Sivik, who claims he's the ruler of the galaxy. We should avoid all risks because I do not trust the Emperor one bit. We could be heading into a trap. We need to safeguard Lena at all costs."

"I understand your meaning, Captain Janus Zephyr," Arcturus said. "I am currently looking out for Lena's best interest. However, we can't let these beings be taken hostage like my people were."

Captain Zephyr looked at Arcturus for a long moment before speaking again. "Once we're done here and get the situation on this planet under control, I'd like to discuss your people and what happened to them in further detail. We're all on the same side here. "

Arcturus inclined his head forward slightly. "I am at your command, Captain Janus Zephyr. I am awaiting further instructions."

Zephyr nodded. "Captain, Captain Zephyr, or Zephyr is fine, Arcturus. You don't have to use my whole name every time you address me."

"Understood, Captain," Arcturus said.

# Chapter 12

## Navaria

## 6552 ASST

Captain Zephyr gathered his crew and said, "We're going to infiltrate a ship under the command of the Intergalactic Star Fleet. This is quite possibly going to start a conflict between us and them." He looked each one of them in the eyes before continuing. "As the fourth child of Maximillian Zephyr, founder of the Stellarnauts, I, Janus P. Zephyr, hereby pledge my fleet to a coming war between the tyrant Emperor, Kraytus Sivik; and his mutated army. If my family does not send forth their fleets to aid us in the coming war, we will stand alone against the Star Fleet. If any of you don't want to be a part of that, please speak now."

*"Mutated?"* Lena mouthed the word.

Everyone looked around at every other member of the crew there. None of them looked as though they were ready to bail. "We're with you, Cap'," Max said, pumping his fist in the air.

"Yes, Lena," Captain Zephyr replied. "The entire Star-Fleet Army is mutated in some way or another. My father and Sivik refuse to work together, denying the Star-Fleet access to Stellarnaut technology. They have delved into a source of power I would never want to endure."

Lena glanced at the captain and then around at the rest of her friends. "What is really going on in the galaxy? Are the Star-Fleet soldiers truly mutants? We must find more about them."

Lena's breathing grew heavier as she contemplated the idea of having to deal with a mutated human.

"Lena!" Emily nearly yelled at the girl. "You must regain control of yourself. I believe 'mutated' was the wrong term to use in this situation." Emily glanced at Max. "Their genes have been altered, granting them advancements in their genetics. The advancements are not unlike what the Zephyr suit does for us. The only difference is our suits; they grant each of us the same advancements. The Star-Fleet, on the other hand, only receives whatever is available at the time. So, in a way, we are all advanced in the same way, but they may be less or more advanced than us."

Lena's breathing lessened as Emily spoke about the Star-Fleet's alterations. Her mind was eased knowing these people weren't mutated monsters that would devour them in an instant. Z's voice brought Lena back to what was going on at hand. "I'm not sure it is the best course of action, but I am not going to stand against you, Captain Zephyr," his static voice sounded pained through the covering of his face.

"I appreciate your honesty and your loyalty, Z," Captain Zephyr said. "Ramirez, once we take this ship, I need you to pilot it back to Ascendant 4. It needs to be docked in the hangar bay. I can pilot the Phoenix once we've finished with the Navarians."

Ava nodded, "I'm sure a Star-Fleet transport ship shouldn't be too hard to learn to fly."

"That's why you're the only one for the job," the captain said.

He turned his attention to Lena and Arcturus. "You two can stand down if you'd like. You're not members of my fleet, and I wouldn't expect you to follow us into such a dangerous situation."

Lena looked at Arcturus, who nodded, "We're definitely in. Arcturus and I don't intend to stand by and let anyone be treated like that, no matter the species."

"That is correct, Captain," Arcturus said. "It would be of great appreciation if, in return, you and your fleet could assist in freeing my people from the enslavement they are currently in."

"Like I said before, I would like to speak with you concerning your people once we're finished here," Captain Zephyr said. "Now, Rodriguez, get an EMP ready; make that two." He turned to Z and Ryan. "I need you two to put your minds together and reverse engineer that portal. I'm sure since they're already on the inside of the ship, it's set to export from the ship, not import."

Z and Ryan both nodded and made their way to the portal. As they approached, a drill-type device appeared in Ryan's right hand. This was something his suit had built into it; she was beginning to understand that each Zephyr suit was equipped with the necessary devices needed for that soldier's specialty. Z's left hand did the same thing. Once Ryan had removed a cover panel, they started working on the wiring and fuses inside the portal's panel.

Lena used her ability to pull on Arcturus's life force. She reached out with her technomancy and started running her mind through the portal's inner workings, trying to see if she could understand what Z and Ryan were doing. Not knowing how she could feel Ryan's hands grabbing the wire she was currently concentrating on. Her mind could feel him release the wire and grab another. It took her breath away when he disconnected a wire and twisted it into another wire. Not understanding what was happening, she pulled her mind from the portal and took a deep breath. Arcturus looked at her and asked, "Are you okay, Lena?"

"I'm fine," she replied. "I was just inside the portal's wiring system trying to see what they were doing, and when they started unhooking wires, it was hard to deal with."

"It is not a smart thing to try to alter a device while it is being altered manually," Arcturus said, a look of worry on his face.

Lena shook her head and said, "I know that now. I won't do it again."

"That would be a good idea," Arcturus said. "We must do more training before you go poking around in any more devices, Lena. Once you are more advanced in the art of technomancy, you will be able to withstand more."

"Okay," she said, then went back to watching them work from afar.

"The soldier with the tracker is moving again, Captain," Emily said. "It appears they have caged or handed off the Xenolian and are heading out for another round."

"Z, Patel, you need to hurry," Zephyr said. "Rodriguez, get ready. I need you to toss those EPMs through the portal as soon as that is ready. Wait ten seconds, then toss the other. Once you toss the second, I'll go through the portal, and I want you right behind me. Chen, you follow Rodriguez. Once we're in, I want Ramirez, Zoravic, and Arcturus to wait ten seconds, then follow us in. Kim, you, Z, and Patel follow them. Zorovic, this will be your first combat encounter. Be prepared to fight if we don't have the room cleared when you enter."

Lena nodded and reached for the revolver at her side. She pulled six bullets from the strap over her shoulder that said "pulse" on them. She removed the laser bullets from the gun and put them in the now-empty slots on her shoulder strap. The pulse shots were then put into the revolver, and she held the weapon at the ready. Not knowing what would happen exactly, she didn't want anything that would kill anyone or damage the ship if she missed.

Z nodded to Captain Zephyr, and with that nod, Max knew what he was to do. The first EMP was tossed through the portal. Emily kept a close eye on her ArmComm, watching for any movement from the soldier with the tracker. Lena counted to herself, "one-two-three-four-five."

"He's been hit," Emily said. "The tracker flew across the room."

"Rodriguez, toss the second one," the captain said.

Max already had it ready; it left his hand before Zephyr finished his order. Lena started counting again, "one-two-three." Captain Zephyr stepped through the portal, gun at the ready. Max went in right after him, and then Emily walked through the portal.

*"One-two-three-four-five-six-seven-eight,"* Lena counted to herself, anticipating the ten-second mark. *"Nine-ten."*

Ava stepped through the portal. Arcturus was on her heels, and Lena followed right behind him. As Lena appeared on the Star-Fleet ship, her eyes scanned the area. Zephyr was engaged with a large man equipped with the same armor as the men they had seen just outside the forest on Navaria. Every time the captain would hit the man, his wounds would heal within a second or so.

Max was blasting at three men on the opposite side of the room. One of them was blown apart as soon as Lena looked that way. Max's weapon had no trouble getting past the Star-Fleet's healing factor. Either that or that one didn't have the same advancements as the one the captain was fighting. Max was hitting right on target because he had a way with his weapons. He locked, loaded, and broke through enemy defenses.

Emily had an ether-lumina blade out. It was like the sword Lena had seen back in the training room, only about half its length. Emily was fighting off another soldier near Zephyr's location. She ran its edge across the man's throat, nearly removing his head from his body. Then she did a backflip, using the momentum of the flip to kick the man under the chin, causing his head to tumble to the floor. That was pretty ruthless, and Lena saw how amazing Emily was in hand-to-hand combat.

Ava's right arm's armor looked like it had transformed into a small pulse cannon, which she was firing at the same group Max was engaged with. The shots were pushing the men back but not stopping them from trying to attack. However, it was giving Max time to power his weapon's ether blast. Shots were fired in all directions, and it seemed that our heroes had an edge over their adversaries. Lena also joined in on the action.

Lena pointed her gun at one of the soldiers who was coming up behind Emily. She aimed down the long barrel of the revolver she'd carried for so long. It took her back to the day her family was killed; all she could think about was how she wanted to use this weapon to kill the man responsible for the death of her family. She wished that man was in front of her and she would not waste a minute taking him down. Shaking her head, she cleared her mind and tried to steady herself. *"I've never even fired a gun. What if I miss and hit Emily? They'll think I did it on purpose because of what happened in the training room that day."* Before she could finish her thought, Emily spun on the soldier, swept his legs out from under him, and then ran the blade of ether-lumina through his chest and out of his back.

Emily looked up at Lena from her squatted position and said, "You can't hesitate, Zoravic. It could be the difference between living and dying. Keep on firing!" Then she turned and went to the aid of Captain Zephyr, who was still fighting the largest of the men on the ship. She jumped and kicked the man in the side of the head, then said, "You have to sever their spine. All their enhancements stem from there."

Zephyr flipped his wrist, and his suit produced the handle of an ether-lumina sword. He activated the weapon as he spun, and a beam of white light protruded from the end of the hilt. The ether-lumina extended about three feet, forming a sword made of pure energy. Captain Zephyr thrust his weapon forward as he spun, running it through the larger man, then cutting to the left, pulling the blade from the man's side and slicing him nearly in two. The momentum of the spin allowed Zephyr to strike down another man. He caught the Star-Fleet soldier between his helmet and chest armor, removing his head from his body. Captain Zephyr was a talented swordfighter, and he impressed his team with his skills. The sword was bursting with energy and slashed through all adversaries.

Lena held her revolver out in front of herself, spinning around to see if there were any other threats in the area. A figure appeared as she looked around, and she pulled the trigger. Ryan was blasted across the room the moment he teleported onto the ship. He hit the wall and fell to the floor.

"Zoravic!" Captain Zephyr yelled. "Lower your weapon; all threats have been eliminated. The coast is clear."

Lena lowered her gun and fell to her knees. She was shaking so badly she could barely hold her composure. Arcturus walked up beside her, knelt, and took her weapon from her hand, sliding it into its holster. She had shot Ryan. *"What have I done?"* she cried to herself. It was a mistake, and she did not know what to do.

Thankfully, Dr. Kim appeared then, and Captain Zephyr said, "Kim, please aid Patel. He's been hit." Dr. Kim went straight to Ryan and started administering first aid to the fallen man.

Ryan was lying against the wall, motionless. *"Did I kill Ryan?"* she asked herself over and over again. Then Ryan sat up and groaned, "I'm glad you loaded that thing with pulse rounds; otherwise, I'd be in a lot more trouble right now. I am more than alive!"

Lena almost laughed when she heard him speak, more from excitement than from finding anything humorous about the situation. She got to her feet and walked over to where Ryan sat against the wall. "I am so sorry. Emily told me not to hesitate, so when I saw someone new, I didn't hesitate." Then she turned and glared at Emily. "You almost caused me to kill my friend, trying to make me a heartless killer like yourself."

Emily retracted her blade and said, "Heatless killer? You think that's what I am?" She walked over to where Lena stood. "No, you're a cowardly little girl who's getting her butt kissed because of who her daddy was."

Lena lunged forward and awkwardly swung at Emily in an attempt to hit her in the face. "Don't say anything about my daddy. He's not here anymore, and you can't talk about him."

"I'm sorry, sweetie, but the truth of it is," Emily said. "He's the only reason you're here and the only reason Captain or any of these others even deal with you."

Lena looked around at each of them, trying to get a reaction out of any of them. "Chen, Zoravic, that's enough. We can't be fighting amongst ourselves while we're in the middle of a combat situation. We need to focus on the situation at hand. We'll continue this discussion later; that's an order. Not another word from you two." Captain Zephyr's voice was loud and stern.

Emily scoffed but turned and walked away. However, Lena said, "No, she disrespected my father and…"

"Lena," Arcturus interrupted. "This is not the time nor the place for this. You must listen to what the captain says right now. Our current situation is one of severe danger."

Lena looked him in the face and said, "I can't believe you're against me too."

"Lena, I am not against you," Arcturus said. "Everyone here is trying to protect you as well as themselves right now. You must not let your anger impede logic."

Without a word, she turned and walked to the other side of the room, sitting down. She put her face in her hands and cried.

Captain Zephyr spoke up after a few moments of silence. "We need to investigate this ship and find the Xenolians. Hopefully, we'll find one who's willing to go with us and show us where their hideout is."

The crew all moved in different directions in search of where they were keeping the surviving aliens. Lena remained seated until everyone left the room except for Arcturus and Captain Zephyr. She looked up at them and asked, "Is it true?"

"No, Lena," Captain Zephyr said. "Chen knows the loyalty your father and I had towards each other, and she's jealous of it. She's my right hand and believes the relationship I had with your father will carry over to you. Chen has been here, at my side, ever since your father left the Armada. Your father was my best friend when he served under me. I never thought he'd ever leave the Stellarnauts, but your mother was something special to him, and he wanted a life with her. Leaving was the only way he could have it."

"I understand that," Lena said. "But I've done nothing to that woman, and she's been nothing but hateful to me ever since she laid eyes on me."

"Lena Zoravic," Captain Zephyr said, a very stern look in his eyes. "I am about to tell you something, but you can never repeat it. Do you understand me?"

"Yes," Lena replied.

Captain Zephyr turned to Arcturus. "That goes for you too, Arcturus."

"I understand, Captain," Arcturus affirmed, nodding his head as though he were one of the humans.

"Emily Chen was in love with your father," Captain Zephyr revealed.

"Are you serious?" she asked incredulously.

"Yes," the captain continued. "I don't know if your father ever pursued her in any way, but I do know she was always in love with him. I think your being here, her knowing that Darian chose another, bothers her. Your presence also reminds her of him."

"I'm glad he didn't choose her," Lena said before she realized she was speaking out loud.

"She's not all that bad," Captain Zephyr said. "I honestly believe she was trying to help you understand combat when she told you not to hesitate. However, you still need proper combat training. That's on me to allow you to come on this mission. It is something we must remedy before you join us on another one."

"I get it," Lena said. "I know I'm just a pain in your side right now. Believe me, I will get better, I will get stronger, and you won't regret bringing me aboard your ship. And... and... Em...Emily," Lena powered through her tears. It was difficult having a conversation about her father, her daddy, without getting emotional. "Emily will see it, too. I'm not just some cowardly little brat that you had to bring along because of my daddy." She had composed herself by the time Emily Chen came back to her mind.

Captain Zephyr nodded. "There's no doubting it," was all he said.

Lena turned to walk out of the room, wanting to see what she could do to help. She was wiping the tears from her eyes when Z startled her. When she opened her eyes again, he was standing right behind her; his one human eye had a look of sadness in it. Not paying much attention to it, she said, "I don't know how long you've been here, but you're not supposed to tell anyone about what you heard. Come on, Arcturus, let's go." Arcturus followed her out of the room.

# Chapter 13

Navaria

6552 ASST

Lena came upon Dr. Kim and Ryan, who had left the room together. They were entering a room near the end of the hall down the center of the spacecraft. She followed them inside. "I've got to apologize to Ryan and thank Samuel for saving him from the potential damage my ignorance could have caused."

When she walked into the room, Ryan was already in one of the cages that held what looked like the same alien who had just been brought aboard the ship. It had the same triangular-shaped head and insect-looking body. The coloring of its outer arthropod shell was the same, too. As she further examined the room, she noticed that every one of them looked the same. Each one had the same size and shape of head, body structure, and color. She opened the door and yelled down the hall, "They're in here! Ryan and Sam found them."

When she turned her attention back to the room, Ryan was staring at her. She couldn't read his expression, *Is he mad at me? It was an accident, I didn't mean to shoot him,* she thought.

"Lena, could you and Arcturus help with getting these cages open?" Ryan asked.

"Yes, of course," Lena replied, not understanding why, but she was overly excited just to hear him speak to her. She turned to Arcturus and said, "Come on, let's see if we can get these cages open."

Arcturus walked close to Lena, getting real close, and said, "These locks are electronic."

"Yeah," Lena said. "We need to try to figure out a way to open them." She started looking around the room for some sort of pry bar, wrench, drill, or anything to help with getting these locks broken.

"Lena," Arcturus said with a stern voice.

"What, Arcturus?" Lena said her mind wasn't there completely, as she was thinking about Ryan and was glad he was up walking around. "I'm trying to find something to open these doors with. Could you please help me?"

"That is what I am doing precisely, Lena," Arcturus replied, a hint of concern in his voice.

Lena turned and looked at him. "Did you find something we can use?"

"Yes," he replied. "You."

"What...?" Then, recognition sparked in her eyes. "I can open them," she smiled, excitement in her tone. "I can open them." Closing her eyes, she concentrated on pulling just enough energy from Arcturus that it wouldn't draw too much attention to him. Then she pushed her mind through the locking mechanisms within the doors. She could feel her mind running across the wires, just like back at the portal. She does not know how or why, but it's like she knows just how to navigate this locking system and how to open it from within. Her mind ran through the integral wiring until she found the wire she was looking for. Following it to the terminal, she looked around until she saw the connector she needed. Then she jumped her mind from one to another, and then the lock popped, and the door opened.

"Wow!" Ryan said, a look of surprise and confusion on his face. "How'd you do that?" Ryan asked, looking at Arcturus.

Arcturus was standing next to a keypad, punching buttons. "I was able to access the mainframe from here. From there, it was just a matter of finding access to the door." He turned and looked at Lena. "I'll try to get the others open as well."

Arcturus punched buttons on the keypads, and Lena would use her abilities to open the rest of the doors in the same manner she opened the first. They worked together, trying to hide her technomancy for now. They would reveal her secret once she has mastered it, but for now, it is essential to keep quiet about it. There is no telling what or how the crew would act if they knew what she was.

Captain Zephyr asked, "Why were they capturing you?"

One of the Xenolians stepped forward and reached out its frontal limb. Across the room, a canister lifted off a countertop and floated over to the captain. Zephyr put out his hands, and the canister was lowered into them. "This is why," a voice came from everywhere, as though each of them was speaking at the same time.

Lena turned, trying to figure out where it was coming from. She wasn't the only one. Ryan, Max, and Samuel all looked around. "They're a hive mind, kids," Z said. Lena wasn't sure she would ever get used to hearing the man speak through his Vox.

"Huh?" Max asked. "A hive mind, what does that mean?"

"They all work and speak in unison," Captain Zephyr said. "They all think what the others are thinking at all times. They speak together, work as one, and have one queen who leads them all. I would say with their combined minds, they could possibly transport a large object with their telekinesis."

"How were they able to get captured if they all think together?" Lena asked. "It seems like if we all had a linked mind, it would be near impossible to corner us and capture us."

"They would have had to get to the queen," Zephyr said.

"You would be correct," the voices came from everywhere again. Every Xenolian in the cabin moved at once in the direction of Captain Zephyr. "You are the leader," the way the voices echoed throughout the ship made Lena feel uneasy. It was difficult trying to pay attention to which one was speaking because they were all speaking. A force such as this would be very hard to debate with, let alone fight. "Could you help us free our Queen?"

Captain Zephyr stood, looked around at each of the Xenolians, and said, "It looks like we need to find and free their queen."

"She has been taken to their leader; another vessel like this one left with her not long before you all arrived," the voices said. "Along with many of our brothers."

Captain Zephyr sat back down and put his face in his hands. "This is going to be far tougher than I thought. We need to get back and speak to the Navarian council leader again."

"We still have many brothers hiding on this planet," the voices said again. "The Navainans allowed us to hide here for our protection. They claim they were subjected to the same treatment many years ago and didn't wish it upon us."

"Those were lying, no-count, big-eared..." Max started ranting before the captain cut him off. "Rodriguez, we'll discuss this with them shortly. There's no need to act out now. I'm sure they have their reasons."

Max nodded and said, "I'm sorry," he looked around the room at all of the Xenolians. "I'm not sure who I interrupted."

"It is quite alright, young Rodriguez," the voices said. "The Navarians have been through something similar to this situation in the past. As you may know, they have a telekinesis power similar to ours. The one extreme difference is the Navarians' power comes from their connection to the core of their planet. We Xenolians get our abilities from within."

"So, you're telling me that the Intergalactic Star-Fleet has been here before conducting experiments on the Navarians, and now they're back trying the same things with you all?" the captain asked.

"Exactly, Captain Zephyr," the Xenolians said all at once again.

"That's why the Navarians called for us," Captain Zephyr said. "They didn't think we'd believe them unless we saw it firsthand."

"Cap'," Max said. "We need to get these Xenolians back to the safety of the rest of their people, or brothers?" He questioned, looking around at them. "Then have that mixed-

172

breed Navarian lead us back to the city and figure out what in the heck has happened here."

When Max said "mix-breed," Lena's heart started beating faster. Had he heard Lyra's confession to her earlier? If he says anything to her, she'll think I told him. Her face must have looked panicked, with sweat forming on it, because Arcturus placed his hand on her shoulder and whispered, "Are you okay?" without anyone else hearing or noticing. Lena nodded her head and continued listening to the conversation.

"I agree," Captain Zephyr said, possibly not catching the mixed-breed comment Max made.

The captain would normally reprimand Max for comments like that. "Can you all get back to your people without our assistance?" He asked the few Xenolians in the room.

"Yes," The voices of the Xenolians came again. "With these soldiers out of the way," they gestured at the Star-Fleet soldiers on the floor. "It should be safe for us to travel alone."

The captain nodded in the direction of the one he had been looking at while speaking to them. "Ramirez, have you learned to pilot this ship yet?"

"Aye, Captain," Ava replied.

"Good," he said. "I want you to pilot this vessel back to Ascendant 4. Take Z, Patel, and the doctor with you. Kim, you need to get Patel to the infirmary and have him checked."

"I'm fine, Captain," Ryan complained.

"That's an order, Patel," the captain's tone was stern. "Aye, Captain," Ryan said half-heartedly.

"What about the girl and her robot?" Emily asked. "I don't think they're needed any further on this mission."

"No, they're staying with us," the captain responded. "Lena has developed a friendship with our Navarian scout. I think her presence will be greatly appreciated by the young Miss. Nova. Arcturus has proven himself useful with electronics if that arises again. With Z and Patel gone, we need someone with his skill on board." The captain had no idea Lena was the one actually unlocking the cell doors, not Arcturus.

Emily scoffed and stormed out of the room. "I'm going to the portal and waiting for you all there."

Lena walked over to Ryan in an attempt to apologize for her earlier mistake. He was engaged in conversation with Z about helping Ava get this ship onto the Ascendant 4 without being shot down by the defenses set up to prevent intruders from boarding the ship. That seemed to be far more important than her feelings about whether Ryan hated her or not.

"Okay," Zephyr said. "Let's go. Ramirez, Patel, Kim, Z, you be safe. We will see you all back on Ascendant 4 soon."

With that, the group split and went their separate ways. Lena couldn't believe she had to leave Ryan without getting the chance to talk to him about what happened and how sorry she was for what she did. Not knowing if he was mad or not was killing her. Ryan is her oldest friend from this crew; he's the one who helped put her in a Zephyr suit, not just any Zephyr suit, her father's old suit. He has done so much to make her feel welcome among the crew. How does she repay him? She shoots him with the very bullets he designed for her gun. "Zoravic," Captain Zephyr said. "Let's go; we need to get back to town and speak with the Navarian leaders about what has happened here today."

She turned to the captain after watching her friend walk in the opposite direction down the hall. She stepped towards the portal, turned, and took one look at where she'd last seen Ryan. Then, she turned and stepped through the portal.

# Chapter 14

## Navaria

## 6552 ASST

Lyra was sitting on the ground with her back against the side of the portal when Lena stepped through it. As soon as Lena appeared, Lyra got to her feet and approached her. Max and Arcturus were already there surviving the area, and Emily stepped through after Lena. Emily headed straight towards the cover of the forest. "You should start moving, Princess." Emily didn't even look at Lena when she spoke to her.

Lyra looked at Lena and asked, "What was that all about?"

"Nothing," Lena replied. "She doesn't like me. However, we managed to free the Xenolians." Lena was eager to share their discovery with Lyra. "We know your people called us here to see firsthand what the Intergalactic Star-Fleet was doing. The Xenolians never were a threat to you all, were they?"

Lyra looked Lena in the eyes and said, "From my understanding, that is correct. Lyraeth devised the whole plan with the other council members. They called upon your Captain directly due to his unyielding reputation in combat and justice, not just for himself or his people but for others as well."

Lena turned to see Captain Zephyr come through the portal, just behind the last of the Xenoilians who had returned to Navaria. "Rodriguez, destroy this portal. I don't want anyone having access to my ship via this device."

"With pleasure, Cap'n," Max said as he turned his large blaster on the thing and opened fire. Make sure not to hit the yellow section where they just came from. Lena could tell he didn't want to accidentally shoot the portal opening and into the ship where the rest of their team was located.

Max's gun leveled the portal, leaving a pile of rubble in the middle of the field. The Xenoilians watched with excitement as it was destroyed. Lena was sure they were glad to know neither they nor any of their other people would be taken through the thing again.

"Thank you," they said in unison before they turned and walked into the forest opposite where Lyra would lead the Stellarnauts back to the city.

"We'll be back," Captain Zephyr yelled to the Xenolians before he turned and followed their guide. "And we'll have your queen to return to you all."

Lena, Arcturus, Emily, Max, and Captain Zephyr all followed Lyra back through the forest, each of them keeping a watchful eye out for any dangerous predators like those they encountered on their way here. Returning to the city was much faster than their journey to the portal where the Xenolians were being transported off-planet. Lena figured it must have been due to the fact that their group was nearly cut in half.

Once they got back to the town, they were escorted back to the main council room, where they had met with Lyraeth and the other leaders of the Navarian people. They found them all sitting at the table in the same places they were when the group had left a couple of days ago. They were greeted with the same hospitality they had received the first time they entered the room.

"Captain Janis Zephyr," Lyraeth said as they entered the room. "What news do you bring of the invading group to my planet?"

"The Intergalactic Star-Fleet?" Captain Zephyr asked. "Why wouldn't you tell me the truth of what was happening here without sending me and my crew on a false mission? My crew could have been hurt or killed going into a situation with false information."

Lyraeth stood. "My people reached out to the Stellarnauts once before about the Intergalactic Star-Fleet and what they've done here before. Your brother, Orion Zephyr, was the Captain who answered our call before. He wanted to hear nothing about Kraytus Sivik and his tyrannical ways. The things that man and his wife did to my people are unheard of. Cutting them open and pulling their innards out to place in their implant devices. The only good thing that came of it was each soldier who received an implant containing Navarian enhancements died as soon as they left the planet. You see, Captain Janus Zephyr, we Navarians have a strong connection to our home. Emperor Sivik found that out the hard way, killing nearly a hundred of his own soldiers before he decided to move on to the next planet, looking for his next advancement.

When we heard the Xenolians were on the run, hiding from the Siviks, we sent out word to have them come here to go into hiding. When we found out the Intergalactic Star-Fleet was closing in on the Xenolians, we called upon you. We needed you to come and look into the matter for yourself. Sivik wants the power of telekinesis more than I want him punished for his crimes against my people." The council leader was yelling at this point, his voice carrying beyond the building. It was clear he was passionate about what he wanted.

"Slow down a minute, please," Captain Zephyr cut in. "You're telling me that my eldest brother, Orion, knew of what happened and did nothing about it? Can you please enlighten me further on this please?"

"Yes, Captain," Lyraeth replied. "Ever since then, we have been looking into your family. You, Captain Janus Zephyr," he emphasized the name Janus, wanting the Captain to know that he was speaking about him directly and not any of the other Captain Zephyrs in the galaxy.

"According to my sources, you are the most honest and honorable man in all of the Stellarnaut Armada. Your sister, Vega, seems to be a trustworthy ally if you need one in the coming war. As for Orion, the Eldest, he is not someone I would trust. Your elder brother, Sol, has been so far out these past years that it has been impossible to get word back from him."

Captain Zephyr chuckled. "You want me to take your word about my family and their loyalties?"

"I would only hope you take what I am saying into consideration," Lyraeth replied. "I know what I say to you now seems difficult to believe. If you seek the truth, it will come to you, Captain Janus Zephyr. I know the name Zephyr is a proud one. It is a name everyone in the galaxy knows and loves. I only hope you keep it that way."

Lena couldn't believe the things she was hearing. Captain Zephyr's eldest brother didn't help these people when they needed it. Now, they had to trick the Captain into finding out the truth about the Intergalactic Star-Fleet on their own. *"Could the ruling empire of the whole galaxy really be that terrible in the way they operate?"*

Lyraeth spoke up once more as he sat back in his seat. "I would also ask that you look into your father's dealings." He looked at Arcturus. "You may be interested in knowing what Maximilian Zephyr has been involved in as well, young Biotan."

Arcturus's eyes opened wide before speaking, "Does Maximilian Zephyr know the whereabouts of my people?"

"The only thing I will say is that it is very important that you convince your captain to look into the matters I have discussed with you all today," Lyraeth said. "My spies are among the best in the galaxy, and I would not go into this light-hearted, Captain."

"We have eliminated your current invading force," Captain Zephyr said. "I cannot promise you that more will not come back here. Your Xenolian companions are still hiding in your forest, and I have promised them I would bring back their queen. I will give you my word as well, counselor. I am going to look into everything you have mentioned here, but there is a personal matter we must deal with first."

"Your word is all I needed, Captain," Lyraeth said. "I know you are good at it. Thank you for hearing me out, and I do apologize for having to be decisive in this matter. It was the only way we thought we could get you to look into the matter. You must understand that our past dealings with the Stellarnaut Armada have been less than pleasant, to say the least. However, I must say that this has been the most pleasant one by far."

"Do not apologize," Zephyr said. "Next time, I would ask that you be upfront with me, though. I feel that we are at that point now. It would always be best that we all remain on the same page at all times because we cannot afford any mistakes now."

"Very well, Captain," Lyraeth said. Along with the rest of the council members, she rose to her feet, and they all bowed as Captain Zephyr and his crew turned and walked from the building. When they reached the Phoenix, and everyone was aboard the ship, the Captain turned to Emily and said, "Now, we discuss the information you received as we left for the forest."

Emily stepped forward and punched some buttons on her ArmComm. She then had her display transferred to the viewing screen in the ship's passenger cabin. A picture of a young woman appeared, accompanied by an article that read:

*Ex-pilot for the Intergalactic Star-Fleet, Maria Rodriguez, was killed in an aerial assault earlier today. It has been reported that she was shot down by the infamous Rogue Stellarnaut, who has been terrorizing the galaxy for the past twenty years. There is no word of any connection between the ex-pilot and the Stellarnaut as of now. Maria Rodriguez, who left the Star Fleet, hasn't lived the most honest life. She was the right-hand lieutenant of the scavenger Jackson Blackwood, aka Black. Blackwood was spotted on Voltorin, the planet where this was all reported to have happened. No one has been able to track him down since then.*

Max lowered his head and started, shaking it back and forth before looking up and saying, "I knew this would happen when she left the Star Fleet for that no-good Blackwood." He turned his attention to the Captain, "We've all been saying it for a year. Now, can we go after this no-good Stellarnaut wannabe?" Then Max lowered his head back into his hands.

"Rodriguez," Captain Zephyr said firmly. "Look up here at me."

Max raised his head and looked at the Captain in the eyes, and tears were beginning to well in his eyes. "Cap'."

"That is the personal task I spoke of back in the council room," Captain Zephyr said. "We are going to Voltorin to hunt down this rogue Stellarnaut. You're right; it's something we should have done when he first surfaced all those years ago."

"What about Blackwood?" Lena chimed in.

"What about him?" Captain Zephyr asked.

"Blackwood and his crew were the ones who killed my family," Lena said. "I didn't put it together before because I figured there are multiple people in this galaxy with the same names, but I'm pretty sure Max's sister is the one who shot my father down just before Blackwood gunned down my mother and brother. I remember Blackwood saying the name Rodriguez over his radio."

Max looked up at Lena and said, "If my sister is the one who killed your father..." He walked over and knelt in front of her. "I want to apologize for her wrongdoings to you. And I want to vow that I will help hunt down and kill her former leader, Jaxson Blackwood, not only for you but for myself. It was because of him that she was ever in that lifestyle. In return, I ask that you help me and my crew track down and take down this rogue Stellarnaut once and for all. I am with you in this, and I feel your pain."

"You have my word, Max," Lena said proudly. She couldn't believe they were about to travel across the galaxy in search of the man who killed her family. *"I love my new friends,"* she thought as Captain Zephyr moved to the cockpit and the Phoenix lifted off, heading back to her new home aboard the Ascendant 4.

# Chapter 15

## Ascendant 4

## 6552 ASST

Captain Zephyr flew the Phoenix just as well as Ava; it was obvious the man had flown many times in his life. They landed smoothly and safely. All of them exited the ship and stepped back onto the Ascendant 4, where they felt more at home than any other place. Even Lena and Arcturus found it comforting being back on the huge transport ship.

"Feels good being back home. Home is where the heart is, and my heart is here," Max said as they walked across the hangar bay.

"It does feel good being back here," Captain Zephyr said. "We have some time to kill; Voltorin is nearly six years away from here. Enjoy this vacation while it lasts."

"How in the hell is that rogue Stellarnaut getting around so much without being intercepted by any of the policing forces in the galaxy?" Max asked. "And do you think it's possible he'll still be there when we arrive?"

"I'm not entirely sure; I would say he'll stay in hiding for a while after making major headlines like that. He cannot afford to pay too much attention to him, but we will hear about him or even from him soon enough. I will not be surprised if it happens before we go to Voltorin or maybe after we get there," Captain Zephyr said.

"Do you think he'll be captured or dealt with by the time we get there?" Max asked. He seemed to be anxious about everything.

"It's possible, but I would say no one wants to tangle with him, and that's why he's still at large. We Stellarnauts have quite a well-known reputation for having a lot to handle. I do intend to find out, though. If I hear that any of my siblings are behind this, I'll kill them myself." The Captain headed for the door. "Chen, accompany me to the bridge. We must set a course for Voltorin."

"Yes, Captain," Emily said, doing all she could to not look Lena's way.

"Zoravic, you and Arcturus should get some rest," the Captain said before they left the room. "You should meet back up with Patel and Z and let them know our intentions and what we've learned from the Navarian leaders."

"Okay, Captain," Lena said, nervous about meeting back up with Ryan. She still couldn't believe she shot him. *"I know he seemed fine when we separated, but I can't help but think he hates me now."*

"Cap's pretty messed up about his brother," Max said. "It's crazy that all this is going on around the same time Orion is apparently going rogue himself, and this rogue Stellarnaut is going around the galaxy wreaking havoc. I'm not saying I think Orion is the rogue, but it is possible he's behind it."

"That's a theory," Lena said. "Better than anything I've thought about. It just doesn't make sense why a Stellarnaut captain, a Zephyr of all people, would be doing shady stuff like this."

"You never can tell about people," Max said. "Look at Blackwood, for instance. Maria and I grew up right down the street from the guy; that's how we know him and how she got wrapped up in everything she was into. He seemed like a decent guy back then, but look what he turned into. I wish she hadn't failed out of the Stellarnaut Academy; she'd be here with us now."

"Yeah, things could have been a lot different," was all Lena said before she and Arcturus left Max and headed toward her sleeping quarters. Lena didn't blame Max for anything that happened, but it made it hard trying to sympathize with him over his sister; she was the one who shot her father down, after all.

As much as Lena enjoyed having her father's suit, she was definitely ready to shed it and get into some comfortable clothing.

*Captain said it would be a few years; I have time to relax in normal clothing,* she thought.

"Would you like to talk about your feelings?" Arcturus asked, trying to sound sympathetic.

"Not really," Lena said. "There's been too much talking today already."

"Very well," Arcturus said. "Don't forget that you have your training sessions with Riddick Shaw in the morning," he reminded her.

"Ahh, that's right," Lena said. "I'd almost forgotten about that. I guess we'd better find Ryan and Z before we get too comfortable."

Lena and Arcturus made their way to the dining hall. After a long journey to the planet's side, getting proper nourishment was next to as important as rest. Surely, that's where Ryan and Z will

185

be. *Ryan more so than Z,* Lena thought. *Does Z even eat?* she asked herself, thinking about it for a second. *He has that mask over his face, but he has to eat something, somehow. Right?*

"Arcturus, does Z eat?" She asked her robotic companion.

Arcturus tilted his head to the side, the same way Kian did when he didn't completely understand what Lena was talking about.

"I am not sure I understand your meaning, Lena," Arcturus responded.

"You remind me of Kian sometimes when you do your head like that," she said, smiling. "I mean, he wears that mask over his face all the time. How does he eat with that thing on?"

"It was Kian who first did that around me; it was my first human interaction in many thousands of years," Arcturus said. "And yes, I understand your meaning about Z's eating now. I believe he eats in his private quarters."

"That's it?" Lena asked. "Does he take the mask off, or is his food ingested through the tubes connected to his mask?"

"I eat in my private quarters because of remarks like that," Z said as he walked around from behind Lena and Arcturus. "My personal choices are no concern of yours, Miss Zoravic. I think it would be wise to keep your thoughts like that to yourself or in your private quarters."

Lena deeply swallowed as he walked by, then turned towards Arcturus and whispered, "I didn't mean for him to hear me." Z was the scariest person on the whole ship, and Lena didn't want to get on his bad side.

"If you do not wish people to hear things you say or ask about them, maybe you should not say or ask things about them," Arcturus responded. He meant no disrespect to Lena; she knew this. However, he did make her feel bad about what she'd said.

"I know, Arcturus," she said, feeling remorseful about her earlier comments. "I was just curious. I wasn't trying to be hateful towards him or anything."

"Perhaps you should address your concerns about the situation with Z," Arcturus said. "I, personally, did not get offended or upset by your line of questions or remarks."

"I know, Arcturus," Lena was starting to get frustrated with the conversation.

"Z is one of the members of the crew that the Captain asked us to inform of the news we learned on Navaria."

"I know, Arcturus," Lena sighed and started after the strange man she was terrified to speak to. She took a few steps towards him before yelling out, "Z?"

Z stopped where he was and turned on his heel. He stood there and waited for Lena to walk all the way to him. It was little things like this that he did that made Lena feel uncomfortable around him. Once she approached him, he said, "Yes, Miss Zoravic?"

"Captain Zephyr wanted me to inform you and Ryan of the information we acquired after parting ways with you all on Navaria."

"Oh, I thought maybe you needed more information on my life habits," Z said quite sarcastically through his vox. "Please, carry on."

"We were heading to the dining hall," Lena said. "If you wouldn't mind, I could talk and walk at the same time. You seemed to be walking in that direction anyway."

"Very well," Z said and turned on his heels once more, continuing on his prior route.

Lena went through all the events of the last leg of their mission, everything after they parted ways. She told him about the Intergalactic Star-fleet and what they did, about Captain Zephyr's family, and everything the Navarians said about them. She also spoke about Max's sister and the rogue Stellarnaut and how they planned on tracking him down for Max.

Additionally, she mentioned their intention to help track down Jaxson Blackwood.

"Rodriguez and I spoke at length about his sister and how the lifestyle she chose to live and how it would cost her her life at a young age," Z said. "I understand his desire to hunt down and get his revenge on the rogue, but why hunt down her old leader? That would be the same as her hunting down Captain Zephyr if something happened to Rodriguez."

Lena sighed, then took a deep breath. "Jaxson Blackwood is responsible for my family's death. He and his crew landed on Zorath near our home, and they were targeted for some unknown reason."

"Blackwood is responsible for Darian Zoravic's death?" Z asked.

"Yes," Lena replied. "And my mother and little brother."

"And seeking this man down is our goal?" Z asked. "Even prior to the mission of tracking down and returning the Xenolian queen?"

"Yes," Lena responded, "Captain says it is nearly six years to Voltorin. I'm sure if we run into any Intergalactic Star-Fleet soldiers between now and then, we'll discuss the matter with them."

"Listen to you?" Z said, "Sounding like a Stellarnaut."

Lena chuckled a bit, then asked. "Do you know where we can find Ryan? I would like to inform him of everything as well?"

"I have Patel working on something very important at the moment," Z said. I will see him soon enough. I will bring him up to date when I see him. Thank you for bringing this to my attention, Miss Zoravic." With that, Z continued down the hall.

*Did Ryan tell Z he didn't want to talk to me? Or is he really working on something for Z?* Lena's mind ran through the different scenarios as she and Arcturus walked the rest of the way to the dining hall. They decided they would go ahead and get some food before they went back to the room for the night. *Am I overthinking things?* she thought again before they entered the hall.

Ava, Max, Samuel, and Emily were all sitting together when she entered the dining hall. Lena went and got a plate of food, then walked over to where they were. Arcturus grabbed a plate as well; though he could eat human food, it was unnecessary for him to do so. Lena thought it made him feel more comfortable with everyone if he was indulging in the same activities they were when he was around.

"Look what the cat dragged in," Emily said when they walked up.

"Hey, Lena, " Ava said. "Max and Emily have been telling us about everything that happened. We didn't know Max's sister was involved with your family's deaths. He has been feeling so bad about it."

"Babe," Max looked at Ava, a look of disdain on his face.

"Ahh, Max," Lena said. "You shouldn't feel bad. You had nothing to do with it." She knew he didn't have anything to do with it, but she would be lying to herself if she said it didn't bother her, knowing it was his sister who shot down her dad.

Max looked up at her, a tear rolling down his cheek. "I know, I can't help it. I never thought Maria was like that. And it pains me knowing she did that to you, to your family."

Lena sat and stared at her food, hating the subject of her family's death. It was comforting knowing she had friends who sympathized with her; she's sure they've all been through losing family and friends. Max was obviously going through it now. Hopefully, in the next few years, both she and Max will have their revenge on the people responsible for their pain.

"Have any of you spoken with Ryan Patel?" Arcturus asked, entering the conversation. "Lena would like to know if he is upset with her?"

Emily laughed, "I'm sure he is. You shot him point blank with an impulse round. Those rounds hurt like hell."

Even Max got a chuckle out of the incident. "I'd almost forgotten about that," he laughed again, a little harder. "She…she…" Laughing between his words. "She blasted his ass as soon as he ported in. Woo…poor guy didn't know what the hell happened. Lena's first time firing a weapon, and she blasts Ryan's ass." He bent at the waist, trying to catch his breath. He'd started laughing so hard that the tears in his eyes were from laughing now.

Lena's head started heating up. "It's not funny," she yelled. "I could have hurt him badly, and you all are just laughing about it."

Max held up his finger. "No, no." He was getting his bearings back. "Those rounds you fired aren't designed to kill. They're meant to detain someone. I think the reason Patel gave them to you is that he didn't want you to accidentally kill someone on your first mission and then beat yourself up about it. He'll be fine, and I'm sure he's not mad at you."

"I really would like to talk to him about it," Lena said. "I know you say he's probably not mad, but I really need to know. Ryan has been my closest friend since I've been here."

"He and Z went to work on something as soon as we landed in the bay," Ava said. "We didn't even have time to talk to them before Z told Ryan they needed to go."

Lena's head dropped; she took a deep breath and sighed. She sat like that for a minute before she looked up and took a bite of her food. After chewing the first bite, she said, "I'm not hungry," then got up and walked from the dining hall.

The next morning, Lena and Arcturus went straight to the training room, where she found Riddick Shaw sitting cross-legged in the middle of the floor. Lena stood there for a minute before she walked over to where he sat. She lowered herself to a cross-legged position and closed her eyes, placing her hands palm up on top of her knees.

Steady breathing was important for this; she inhaled deeply through her nose, then exhaled slowly out of her mouth. Her mind needed to be clear of her surroundings. She thought about the day her parents first brought Kian home from the hospital. He was such a tiny little thing, and Lena was so terrified he would get hurt if she didn't keep a watchful eye on him at all times. She stayed near him for the first several days after coming home; her mother tried to get her to go play or to do something with her father. But Lena wouldn't have it; she wanted to be there to protect Kian.

Within a few moments, she opened her eyes and found herself in the vast nothingness she had experienced before they left for their mission. "Lena!" Kian's excited voice yelled. There he was, her little brother, or the essence of him anyway, standing there looking at her with a smile on his face.

Lena's eyes went wide before she mouthed the word "Kian."

"We've been waiting for you to come back," Kian said.

She couldn't believe what she was seeing. The silhouette of a woman was walking up behind Kian. It was that of a woman. Could it be? "Mom? Is that you?" Her voice broke.

"Welcome back," her mother's voice said. "I am sorry, Lena. Sorry, we left you alone; sorry for the last words between us."

"I know," Lena cried. "Me too; I am sorry, Mommy. I miss you so much."

The essence of her little brother came close and wrapped his corporeal arms around Lena's legs. "Come see us again, Lena," Kian said. Then the figures dissolved into nothingness, and Lena was once again sitting cross-legged in the middle of the training room floor. Looking around, she couldn't figure out what had just happened. There were tears running down her face as she looked around.

Riddick Shaw got to his feet and nodded for Lena to grab one of the bow staves leaning against the walls. He had already gotten one for himself. "What just happened?" she asked the mute man.

He nodded towards the staff, who were leaning against the wall once again. Tears were still rolling down her cheeks. *"Had it been a dream?"* she asked, squaring off with her trainer. They bowed to each other, and then their combat training commenced. By the end of the session, Lena was worn out; her body was, anyway. Her mind, however, was clear and alert, and she felt pretty good overall. She wrote off the vision she'd seen during her meditation session as a dream; there's no way it could have been anything other than that.

When she exited the training room, Ryan was walking down the hall, his back already turned to her. Instinctively, she yelled, "Ryan." She covered her mouth. At this point, she had no idea what to say to him. *"I should have just gone the other way. I don't know if I want to deal with this right now. Please don't let him be mad at me."*

Ryan turned, and with a big smile on his face, he said, "Lena! I haven't seen you since you've gotten back." His facial expression changed when he got closer to her. "You stink," he laughed. "Riddick worked you hard today, I take it?"

"Yeah, I just finished a long training session," she said. "I'm definitely in need of a shower." She made a gesture as if to smell herself by lifting her arm and turning her nose to her armpit.

"Brutal," Ryan said. "I'm sure he's making things rough, considering you bailed on him right after signing up with him."

"It was definitely a tough training session," Lena said. "I

was about to get a shower and go recover for a bit. But when I saw you, I had to get your attention. I've been looking for you ever since we got back. I need to apologize for what happened back on the Star-Fleet ship. I froze up at one point, and Chen got onto me about it. So, the next thing I knew, you ported in right in front of me, and I shot. I'm not ready for combat, not in the least. Riddick is teaching me to fight, but I need to train with Max or someone on combat scenarios or something like that. I'm sorry I'm ranting because I'm scared that if I stop talking, you'll tell me you hate me."

Ryan smiled. "You're fine, Lena. Don't worry about it. It was an honest mistake. It knocked me silly for a few minutes, but no harm was done. Plus, if you had hit me with something more devastating, Sam was there. He was combined with a Zephyr suit, and no one on that mission was in any real danger. Unless Sam was taken out, that is." Ryan's expression changed once again to one of seriousness. "Keep that in mind, Lena. Always keep the doctor safe on any missions you ever go on. If the doctor goes down, don't get me wrong, the Zephyr suits are awesome, but they take time to heal major wounds."

Lena's body was tingling all over. She couldn't believe he wasn't mad. She was so excited she couldn't hold back her smile. "Thank you, Ryan." She reached out and gave him a big hug.

"I've thought you were mad at me this whole time. I've been stressed out about it so badly. Ryan, I really thought you hated me."

"Lena, I could never hate you," he said. "As silly as it sounds, you're like my best friend here. I know you haven't been here long, but I feel like I have a strong connection to you."

"Same," she said. "You are the best friend I have, and I can't lose you."

"I thought I was your best friend, Lena," Arcturus said. He was standing behind her during Ryan's conversation with her.

"Ahh, Arcturus," Lena said. "You are my best friend, too."

"You should have come to see me," Ryan said as he looked between Lena and Arcturus.

"I tried," she replied. "I've talked to Z about where to find you; Max, Ava, and even Emily were there. I really did try to find you, but everyone said you were very busy with something Z had you doing."

"Oh, yeah, that," Ryan said. "He's been having me work on some new addition to the suit he's hoping to have working before we get to Voltorin."

"What is it?" Lena asked, curiosity peeking in her mind now.

"I can't talk about it right now," he replied. "I'll get into trouble if anyone finds out. Z's very personal about things like that. If he has an idea, he never lets anyone know about it until it's done. He doesn't want anyone getting excited about something and then being disappointed if it doesn't work out."

"That's understandable," Lena said.

"Yeah, but everything he's ever worked on has been a success," Ryan said. "The man's brilliant."

"Do you think your current statements line up, Ryan?" Arcturus asked.

"What do you mean?" Ryan asked.

Lena looked at him with her head tilted down, her eyes rolled up, and a smirk on her face. "Come on, Ryan, think about it. If Z doesn't talk about his ideas unless they're successful..." She paused for a long second before finishing, hoping he would catch on to what she was saying. "No one probably knows about his failures."

"Precisely," Arcturus said.

Ryan's eyes slowly widened as recognition sank in. "You're right; I never thought about it that way. The man has possibly had more failed attempts at things than successes."

Lena laughed as she and her friends walked down the hall. Ryan escorted her to the shower before he went on his way to work on whatever it was Z had him working on. Her mind was clear of any bad feelings from Ryan; now she was free to concentrate on her training, and that's what she did moving forward.

# Part 3

# Chapter 16

Ascendant 4

6558 ASST

Lena had spent the past few years aboard the Ascendant 4. She trained under Riddick Shaw, becoming one of the most consistent combatants he had ever trained. Many long days were spent with Max in computer-simulated combat situations, something she felt she needed training on due to the incident on Navaria. She and Arcturus spent many late nights delving into the inner workings of the ship's technological components. Lena's technomancy abilities had grown nearly as much as her combat skills. But nothing had prepared her for the next announcement she received on her ArmComm.

When the chime sound "beeped" on her forearm, she looked at the display screen:

*Attention crew members of Ascendant 4. We are approaching Voltorin. Please make any and all necessary arrangements before we dock in the spaceport. We will be going planetside in less than one week. Thank you.*

*Specialist Emily Chen.*

Lena's heart almost leaped from her chest at the announcement. *"Am I ready?"* she asked herself, something she'd done several times over the past five and a half years. *"Will Blackwood be there? Will the rogue still be there? Has everything she and her friends done over the past years been for nothing?"* The questions rang through her mind as the announcement sang through the halls of the ship once again.

Emily must have sent out the message prior to leaving her office because Lena turned a corner, and there, the small female soldier was walking down the hall. She was poking at the screen of her ArmComm. *Is there nothing she can do besides poke at her screen?* Lena thought.

"Chen," Lena greeted Emily as she approached.

Emily looked up. "Zoravic," was all she said before she looked back at her ArmComm and continued down the hall. Lena hadn't seen or heard much from Emily over the past few years. Emily stuck to her work with the Captain and gathered information about what was going on around the galaxy. Lena and Emily hadn't had any crosswords since their trip to Navaria.

There haven't been many sightings of the rogue Stellarnaut in the last few years, either. Any sightings have all still been on or around Voltorin, which leads Captain Zephyr and the rest of the intelligence to believe he still has business on Voltorin.

Lena's only concern is that Jaxson Blackwood has fled the planet, and they won't be able to find him when they get there. Arcturus believes Blackwood may still be in the area because there have been reports of multiple Spectre-class fighter ships built and purchased from a supplier on Voltorin. "It was Jaxson Blackwood's ship of choice, if you remember, Lena," he would say, trying to keep Lena's hopes alive. He wasn't wrong. Lena remembered her father shooting down several Spectres before he was shot down himself. Even after all these years, she still can't believe he's gone — him, her mother, and her father. It is so surreal, and thoughts continue racing in her mind about what could have been or how her life would be different if all of them were alive. It was a very bitter pill to swallow. She had built a very thick skin to go on, and that too because she wanted to go on and fight for them. She knew this was what they would have wanted her to do, and she was living for them. She strongly felt that her family was watching over her from whatever heaven they were in and looking out for her. Several tears ran out of her eyes, and she remembered her father once telling her, "My darling Lena, when you feel like crying, never hold back the tears. If you do not release them, they shall stay inside forever, and the pain will last longer. Once you release them and you have cried your heart out, your pain shall be gone forever. Grief should never become a burden, so let it go with your tears, my child."

Lena then reached inside her backpack and pulled out the photo of her father, holding it close as she had been doing regularly for the past few years. Alongside, she retrieved the letter her mother had left on her bed, tears welling in her eyes each time she read the words on the parchment.

She would also get out of Kian's small handheld video game system and play the games he had on it. Whenever she played games on the game system, she felt like her father was playing with her because they would always play video games together when she was younger. Some evenings, she and Arcturus would spend hours playing together. It still amazed her how well the ether-lumina produced by the Stellarnauts kept the system running nonstop without needing to charge it.

She kept all these items inside her backpack, something she would take with her if anything ever happened. She didn't want to have to spend time packing them back away if she ever did have to leave. She found the Ascendant 4 just as much a home as she did her home back in Zorath these days, but she never felt like she was really a Stellarnaut. She was the only member on the ship who had a Zephyr suit but didn't earn it by going through the academy. Even though she hadn't worn her father's suit in a few years, more so to age a little more than not wanting to wear it, There was nothing worse to Lena than being sixteen for twenty-something years. She wanted to get to at least her twenties before she decided to wear the suit full-time like most other Stellarnauts do.

*I need to go get my suit out and clean it up. It seems like I'll be suiting up and going planetside within the next week or so,* Lena thought.

"Arcturus, I just got a message," Lena said, her voice sounding much more mature. "We're approaching Voltorin. We need to get my Zephyr suit out and get ready for a mission planetside."

"That is great news, Lena," Arctiris replied. "We must also go speak with Ryan Patel and Max Rodriguez. I am more than certain they will be excited about the news of Voltorin's approach."

"Yeah, I would like to reassure Max that we're here for him," Lena said. "I know I want to get Blackwood just as much as he does the rogue, but I want him to know we don't intend to back out on our promise."

"You use the term 'our' as though I was involved in your promise to Max Rodriguez about neutralizing the rogue Stellarnaut," Arcturus said in a matter-of-fact manner. "I do wish to join you all on your mission planetside. I merely wanted to point out the fact that I did not, however, promise Max Rodriguez anything."

"You're too much, Arcturus," Lena said, laughing at her oldest friend. "You know you don't have to keep calling everyone by first and last name. It's just like calling Captain Zephyr just Captain. You can just say Max, and I will know who you're talking about."

"I know, Lena," Arcturus said. "I respect Captain Zephyr, and I respect you. That is why I use your names the way I do. If Max Rodriguez earns my respect, I will call him Max."

"I know, I've heard this all so many times before," Lena said. "I just don't understand why you don't have enough respect for my friends to call them by just their first name."

"It is not for you to understand, Lena," Arcturus said firmly.

"Okay, okay, I'll drop it," Lena said. "But, either way, let's go find them, then we can get the Zephyr suit ready."

They left the training room where Lena had just finished her morning training session with Riddick Shaw. On their way to the barracks, where she was sure she would find Ryan and Max, they ran into Z.

"Miss Zoravic," Z said as she neared him. "I am looking for Patel. Have you seen him this morning?"

"No, Z," Lena responded. "Why does it seem like every time I'm looking for Ryan, so are you? Do you keep tabs on me to interrupt my search or something?"

"Do not be ridiculous," Z responded. "I am always in search of Patel; he is my assistant, and I constantly have tasks for him to complete. Just now, I received a message that we are approaching Voltorin. It is imperative that Patel and I have everything in order before we depart for the surface."

After six more years of living on this ship and encountering Z on numerous occasions, Lena still hasn't gotten used to how Z looked. She believes she will always be frightened of his appearance.

"If I run into him before you find him, I will send him your way," Lena said.

"I could assist you, Z," Arcturus offered.

"Thank you, Arcturus," Z responded. "But this is the stuff that Patel and I have been working on for some time. I need his assistance for now."

"Understood," Arcturus said to the man he'd taken a liking to over the years and nothing more.

"That is something I respect about you, Arcturus," Z said before he left. "You understand the importance of one's task and don't push to find out more."

Lena was glad Z spoke up. She was able to ask what they had been working on. She would have looked quite the fool had she started before Z did. She and Arcturus continued to the barracks once they parted ways with Z.

They found Max and Ava sitting in a lounge area in the center of the barracks quarters. The two were close, whispering to each other. When Lena and Arcturus walked up to them, Lena said, "Did you all get the alert?"

Max looked up, a smile on his face. "We did. You have no idea how happy I am right now. It's still common knowledge that the rogue is still here."

"Yeah," Ava said. "I just hope we don't have any issues finding him. We already have too many issues to deal with."

"Voltorin isn't a very big planet," Lena said. "Everything I've read about it says it's about half the size of Zorath, and Zorath isn't very big either."

"Yeah," Ava said. "But it's a central hub for trade, and it has the biggest suppliers of goods in most of the galaxy. The only planet that ever did more was old Earth in the Sol System. But Earth is mostly desolate these days. The only people who stay there are those who work with Maximilian Zephyr in the facilities where he creates the ether-lumina."

"I have read that the planet is almost one big city," Lena said. "But shouldn't it be easy to track down their last known locations? Surely, you all have contacts in the city who have information on the comings and goings on the planet."

"Yes," Ava said. "Captain Zephyr spent a lot of time on Voltorin as a young man. It was his father's rule. Before any of his children were able to travel the galaxy at the helm of their ship, they had to spend ten years on Voltorin and learn the ins and outs of how the galaxy works. If you want to learn about people and other species in the galaxy, this is the place to go."

"I heard the planet is inhabited by multiple species from around the galaxy," Lena said.

"That is correct, Lena," Arcturus said.

"Thanks, Arcturus," Lena said. "But anyways, I came to see you all and Ryan. Have you seen him this morning?"

"Yeah, he was in the dining hall this morning getting breakfast," Ava said.

"Actually, come to think of it," Max chimed in. "He said he was going to see you once he got done eating. So, he might be heading out towards the training area. He probably thinks you're still there."

"Okay, I'll head back out that way," Lena said. "I'll see you two later."

Lena and Arcturus left the barracks and headed back to where they had just come from.

On her way down the halls, she saw Captain Zephyr and Emily heading her way. Emily was punching information into her ArmComm as the Captain was speaking. Lena wasn't close enough to hear what he was saying, but it must have been important because Emily was typing faster than she'd ever seen anyone type before.

"Good morning, Captain," Lena said when they were close enough to engage in conversation.

"Ahh, Miss Zoravic and Arcturus," the Captain said when he looked up. "My two favorite passengers. How have you all been? Haven't seen much of you lately?"

"Same old stuff, Captain," Lena said. "Train, train, train. Life on a Stellarnaut ship is pretty much just that."

"There are recreational facilities as well," Emily chimed in.

"Yeah, I know," Lena said. "We hit them up from time to time. I am old enough to drink now but still haven't found the courage to try any of the drinks."

"Yes," Captain Zephyr noticed. "You have let yourself age; I can see it now. Don't get too used to leaving that suit off, though. You'll end up like Z. I know it's hard to tell, but Z aged a lot before his accident. His ether-lumina-powered eye helps with his aging now. He has no choice but to stay young. You know, my brother once told me before Z was transferred here and before his accident that the man never wore his Zephyr suit. Sol said he thinks the man was trying to get old and die."

"That's sad," Lena said. "Maybe life as a Stellarnaut isn't suitable for everyone. I know it could be a hard decision, but if the man wants to grow old and die, why don't you let him? It is his life and his choices. We should not intervene with his decisions."

"Well," the Captain said. "I don't believe he wants to. I'm not saying he never did, but now I just don't get the vibes from him like I used to."

"Yeah, well. He freaks me out," Lena said. "I don't know what it is, but he just always seems to be there. Plus, he looks scary as hell."

Captain Zephyr and Emily both laughed. "I can't allow a member of my crew to die just because he's scary-looking, Lena," Captain Zephyr said. "Not to mention, I believe he's the best engineer in the entire fleet, counting every other ship and crew in the galaxy."

"I know, Captain," Lena said. "There's just something about him that sends me into chills from time to time."

"Either way," Captain Zephyr said. "We must get going. There are many plans to be made before we reach Voltorin's docking station. We will hopefully dock within the next few days. You need to get any affairs in order before we go planetside."

"Yes, sir," Lena said before they started back down the halls. "Oh," she yelled back over her shoulder. "Have you seen Ryan?"

"Who?" Zephyr asked.

"Patel," Arcturus corrected.

"No, not for some time now," Captain Zephyr said. "You might check with Z. If I recall, Patel is Z's right-hand man."

"Thanks, Captain."

Lena and Arcturus continued their search for Ryan. She was almost tempted to use her ArmComm to reach out, but that was against the rules unless it was an urgent call or message that needed to be relayed. They got back to the training room, and Lena stuck her head inside. Riddick was still there; he had another trainee. But Ryan was nowhere to be seen inside the room. Maybe it wasn't meant for her to see Ryan today.

"Arcturus, I think we should just go back to our room," Lena said. "I need to get showered, and I need to get my Zephyr suit ready. We can't spend all day looking for Ryan."

"That is an excellent idea, Lena," Arcturus said. "I was going to suggest it myself once we parted ways with Captain Zephyr and Emily Chen."

"Why didn't you?" she asked.

"Because you would have declined," he responded. "How do you know I would have?"

"Lena, you have been my closest friend for more than thirty years," Arcturus said.

"Twenty-five of them, you slept. However, in the past six years, I have observed you very closely. From my understanding of how your mind thinks. You would not have given up your search for Ryan without first looking here." He nodded to the training room door.

"You're probably right," she said. "Come on, let's go. I have to get a shower."

# Chapter 17

Ascendant 4

6558 ASST

When Lena got out of the shower, she grabbed her Zephyr suit and pulled it on. The suit formed to her body, and then it tingled all through her. She hadn't put it on in nearly six years; it had to reform itself and repair anything it found wrong or damaged with Lena's biology. Once the suit completed its full-body scan and stopped tingling, she went to the shelf where she kept her armor and pulled it off piece by piece, cleaning each item before she attached it to the suit in its appropriate spot.

When she finished gearing her suit up, she reached over and grabbed the revolver from the top shelf. It was a beautiful weapon, one she loved and hated at the same time. She'd spent so much time over the years training herself on firing and loading the weapon. After shooting Ryan with it, it took some time for her to feel comfortable picking the thing up again. But now she was able to fire all six rounds in just a couple of seconds and reload it almost as fast. She'd told herself over and over again that once she put a bullet in Jaxson Blackwood's head with the thing, she would personally destroy it - a fitting end to the weapon for all the pain it's caused her over the years.

Once the weapon was properly cleaned, she holstered it. She ran her mind through the lighting system in the room, flipping the switch off while at the same time working the mechanism that operated the door locks. The lights went out, the door opened, and she and Arcturus walked from the room and headed to the hangar bay. It was time to get a look at the Phoenix they would be boarding when it was time to leave this ship.

When they arrived at the bay, the Intergalactic Star-Fleet ship they had commandeered back on Navaria was still in the hangar. It was mostly dismantled, but it was still there all the same. Max and Ava were both already in the hangar. Max, of course, was outfitting the ship with the latest upgrades he'd made to the heavy weapons system on their ship. Ava, on the other hand, was making sure all the vital parts and fluids were in tip-top order, as she would say.

"Lena," Ava said as they approached, "Check you out, back in action! Wow! I haven't seen you in your suit in years, it seems."

"Yeah," Lena replied, "It's been a while since I've suited up. Had to let myself age a little. I couldn't be sixteen forever, you know. Plus, it gave Arcturus and Ryan time to make some improvements to the old thing."

"Hopefully, they added some decent weaponry to that dinosaur," Max interjected. "That second-gen suit has always needed major upgrades. That's why they came out with the third-gen suit anyway. The suit was a good design when it was created, but Zephyr knew there was so much more he could do, and bam," he motioned to his suit, "he created the greatest thing this galaxy has ever seen. The third-gen Zephyr suit—well, I kinda guess they've seen it now, but you know what I mean." He then went back to bolting a rapid-fire plasma blaster to the undercarriage of the ship.

"This mission is going to be one of the most personal missions Captain Zephyr has ever run before," Ava said. "It's been exciting thinking about being able to get out there and take down someone who's not only given us, The Stellarnauts, a bad name but also hurt my babe so badly." She walked over, leaned under the Phoenix, and kissed Max on the side of his head.

*I understand our main mission here is to take out or capture the rogue Stellarnaut. I just hope everyone remembers that Blackwood is supposed to be here too, and he's just as much of a priority to me as the rogue is to Max,* Lena thought as Ava was going on about the rogue Stellarnaut.

"Thanks, babe," Max said, never missing a beat with his wrenching.

"Is it okay if I go ahead and load my bag on the ship, Ava?" Lena asked.

"Yeah, absolutely," Ava said. "Just put it in the back. I'm sure the Captain and his sidekick will be here loading their stuff later, too. And you know how Miss Pricy gets if she doesn't get her space in the front."

"Yeah, I know," Lena said. "Thanks, I've still got to find Ryan. He's one of the hardest people to find on this ship."

"Oh, Ryan was with Z earlier," Max said. "They were going to Z's lab. He said they had some last-minute adjustments to make. It will all be taken care of." He shrugged his shoulders in a gesture. Lena knew not to ask what they were making adjustments to because Max had no clue.

"Thanks," Lena said one last time before leaving the hangar. "I'll see you two in a couple of days when we finally get off this ship for a few days. Till then, take care!"

"Un-huh," Ava said, her head back under the hood of the ship. Lena hated it when Ava was working on the ship. It always reminded her of the time she spent in her father's shop while he had his head under the hood of someone's ship.

Arcturus led the way to Z's lab, a place he'd spent almost as much time in as he had her living quarters. Lena believes Z is just as important to Arcturus as she is sometimes. She hates how much time he spends with the scary old man. Z could be a bad influence on Arcturus, and Lena would hate to see Arcturus turn into a self-loathing hermit who does nothing but boss his pupils around and sneak up on people when they least expect him.

"Do you know what Z and Ryan have been working on?" Lena asked Arcturus.

"I have been given limited access to their project," Arcturus said. "However, I have given them a few minor thoughts on the project. I hope it makes sense to them. I deeply analyzed it."

"What?" Lena asked. "You do know what they're working on? Why haven't you told me before?"

"You never asked before," Arcturus said matter-of-factly. "Not to mention, Z asked that I say nothing to anyone about the project. He is not certain it will work correctly or not."

"I can't believe it," Lena laughed. "Duped by my best friend, sigh!"

"I am sorry, Lena," Arcturus said.

"Don't be sorry, Arcturus," she said. "I'm not mad at you. I'm honestly glad. It makes me happy that you don't share other people's personal stuff with others. It lets me know my secrets are safe with you. I am very glad that I can trust you."

He looked at her and then asked, "Did you not think prior to this encounter that your secrets were safe in my possession?"

"No, I've always trusted you, Arcturus," she said with a smile on her face. "This is just, kinda..." She paused for a second, thinking of the right word. "Like reassurance. It would be hard not to trust someone who lets you siphon their life's energy from them."

"That does make good sense," he said. "We are here." He stopped in front of Z's door.

They had been talking so much that Lena hadn't even realized they'd already made it. She walked up and knocked on the door.

"Yes," she heard Ryan's voice from inside the room. "It's me and Arcturus," she yelled through the door.

"Of course it is," Z said, obvious frustration in his voice. Even through the static, Lena could still tell if he was annoyed or not. It could be that he always seemed annoyed.

The door opened, and Ryan stood there. "Come in," he said. "Haven't seen you for a few days. How have you been?"

"I'm good," she replied. "Been looking for you for a few days. Did Z not tell you I was looking for you?"

Ryan turned and looked at Z. "It slipped my mind," the half-robot-looking man looked guilty.

"Of course you did," Ryan said, laughing at the man. "What is the deal with you not wanting me and Lena to hang out?"

Z just turned back to his desk and started going through the papers, trying to find some important documents.

"I don't know what his deal is," Ryan said. "So, what's up?"

"I was just wanting to see you about the message we received the other day about Voltorin. I knew how excited everyone was about it. I saw Max and Ava and wanted to see you about it, too."

"Yeah, Z and I have been working nonstop trying to get the—" "Patel, keep quiet about it," Z cut in.

"I know, I wasn't going to say anything," he said. "We're not sure it's even going to be ready for this mission, but we'll give it our all."

"Either way, I'm sure it'll be great once it's done," Lena said. "I just wanted to say it seems like everyone is so hung up on getting the rogue Stellarnaut. But...but, it's possible my family's killer is still here too. I just," she started crying, holding one hand out and the other over her face. Once she got her composure back, she started again. "I just don't want anyone to forget about getting him, too, but it seems like everyone is so concerned about the rogue that Blackwood is just a distant memory to them. Blackwood is as much a priority as the rogue. We must never forget that."

"Lena," Ryan stepped in and took her hands. "I assure you that no one here has forgotten about the man who took your family. Certainly not me, and I promise you, Max hasn't forgotten what his sister did to your dad, and he intends to see his promise through, too. We are all on the same team, so never forget that. I understand your concerns, and I assure you that we will not let you down. You are an integral part of our team, and your wishes are very well known."

Lena smiled at that. "Thank you, Ryan." She leaned in and kissed him on the cheek. "You have always been here for me, and I want you to know how much I appreciate it. All of what you said sincerely means a lot coming from you."

"Lena," Ryan said, holding his hand to his cheek where she kissed him. "Don't worry about it, you're my best friend. Plus, you'd do the same for me."

"That's quite enough," Z said from his chair. "Miss Zoravic, you and Arcturus can show yourselves out. Patel and I have much work to do. We will see you two in a couple of days when it is time to go planetside. Until then, you must leave us to our work."

Lena did not stick around much longer once Z got to the point of kicking her out of his lab. She just hoped Ryan wouldn't face any backlash for her visiting him there.

*But Ryan's right; Z never lets him get out to see me. That's why I always have to see him in the lab,* she thought. And he better not give Ryan a hard time about it.

The next morning, Lena went to her last training session before she would be leaving to go planetside. Riddick knows this break is coming; he's already penciled her off his schedule for the next week after today. When she walked into the training room, Arcturus was right behind her, and Riddick was standing in the middle of the floor, completely decked out in his Zephyr suit, along with his ether blade at the ready. Lena, knowing her suit was now equipped with an ether blade, engaged hers and then stepped to Riddick, eager to see how well she could wield an actual ether blade, considering she'd been practicing with a wooden staff up to this point.

Lena bowed to her trainer, who bowed in turn. Riddick smiled just enough for Lena to see before his facial features morphed back to the serious and stern expression she was accustomed to. She smiled to herself and stepped forward, her blade swinging around. Riddick caught her blade with his own, deflecting her back a step. *He was bigger and stronger. I need to engage him in a way that causes his strength to work against him,* Lena thought.

She stepped in again and made to swing around the same as before. Just as she expected, he stepped in to block her blow and sent her backward again. Lena, however, had a different plan. As soon as he stepped in and his blade started moving forward, she disengaged her ether blade and ducked his swing. This caused his momentum to continue forward. Then she swept his feet out from under him. Riddick tumbled forward. Lena re-engaged her ether blade and stepped on his back, the blade pointing at the back of his head. Riddick disengaged his ether blade and tapped the floor.

Riddick got to his feet and bowed to her once again. For a man who never speaks, he has a way of communicating with Lena that lets her know he's proud of her. He then motioned for her to have a seat as he took one himself. Crossing his legs, he put his hand atop his knees, palm up, and closed his eyes. Lena followed his lead, sitting with her legs crossed and palms up. She looked at Riddick and smiled as she closed her eyes. Kian was the first person to come to mind, just like always when she meditated with Riddick. He was following her around their father's shop while she gathered items for her next explorations.

"Tan I doe wit you sissy?" Kian asked when she threw her backpack over her shoulders.

Lena bent over and kissed Kian on the forehead. "When you get a little older, I'll take you on all my journeys out into the world, little brother," she whispered.

Lena opened her eyes to the vast nothingness she always found herself in during her meditations with Riddick. The same silhouette stood before her. "You have come a long way. You are ready for the task ahead of you."

"How do you know?" she asked, knowing she wouldn't get an answer in return.

The silhouette started fading out. Before it was completely gone, it said, "The Biotan is the key."

She opened her eyes, once again, back in the training room. Riddick had already gotten to his feet and walked across the room, making marks in the schedule on the wall. What in the hell was that all about? "The Biotan is the key?" she mused. She looked over at Arcturus, sitting on the same bench, doing the same thing he always did: looking around the room.

Lena and Arcturus left the room. While they walked, Lena asked Arcturus, "What do you do while Riddick and I meditate?"

"I speak to Chronotech," he answered.

*"Is the silhouette Chronotech?"* she asked herself. I'll worry about it later. I have to get ready for Voltorin. "Does he speak back to you? she asked.

"No, not in the sense you mean," Arcturus answered.

Lena and Arcturus met with the rest of their crew in the hangar the next morning.

Everyone was there, and the whole crew was back together again. Z and Ryan were the last to arrive. Once they got there, everyone loaded up in Ava's Phoenix. Captain Zephyr stood as the ship started to lift off.

"I feel like I should tell all of you who have never been to Voltorin before it's not like any other place you've ever been. The cityscape is larger than any city that ever stood on old Earth. There are more alien species living on this planet than most of you know. The crime rate is astronomical. We're not here to solve that issue, and I just thought I should point that out. Don't intervene in Voltorin police business; we police the galaxy, not the planets." He sat down and looked around the ship, meeting each and every one of them in the eyes before he spoke again.

"Everyone, be careful and watch everyone's backs. This place is dangerous." He sat back, and Ava took them down to the surface of the planet where Lena would possibly get her revenge for her family's death.

# Chapter 18

Voltorin

6558 ASST

The lights emanating from the surface of the planet were exhilarating. Lena had never seen anything so beautiful. It was like peering out into the galaxy and witnessing all the stars condensed into one compacted area. The entire planet's surface was adorned with sparkling lights, stretching as far as her eyes could see. Her face was plastered against the porthole window, and her mouth dropped open as she gazed at the sight.

"You okay there, Lena?" Ryan asked, smiling at her reaction to the sight.

Lena shook her head, tearing her gaze away from the mesmerizing sight to look at Ryan. "It's breathtaking," she said. "Come take a look."

Ryan slid over to where Lena was looking through the window. His eyes widened in amazement as he took her place, looking through the window. She placed her hand on his shoulder and looked over it to get one last look at the city lights before they got too close. He looked up at her and smiled once again at the look of wonder on her face. Ryan reached up and placed his hand on top of hers.

Lena looked down at Ryan, the big smile still on his face. "What?" she asked.

"The way you smile," he said. "It makes me smile too."

"Why?" she chuckled.

"Because when I first saw you, you were a lost girl who had just had her whole world pulled out from under her," Ryan said. "I know everything you were seeing on the Ascendant 4 was so fascinating, but you couldn't enjoy it because of how torn your world was. And now, to see that look of amazement on your face, it makes me happy."

Lena's face flushed red for a second before she heard Ava's voice come from the front of the ship.

"Everybody, get ready. We are approaching our landing site," Ava shouted over her shoulder.

"Listen up," Captain Zephyr said. He was standing in the walkway of the Phoenix's small passenger bay. "When we land, we will be separated into two groups. I'll lead one group, and Z will be in charge of the second. Ramirez, Chen, and Patel will come with me. Rodriguez, Kim, Zoravic, and, of course, Arcturus will come with Z."

The two groups looked around at their assigned group and leaders.

*Why did he have to stick me with Z? Is he trying to get me to like him or something?* Lena thought. *Well, at least we have Max. At least I know I'll have someone watching my back.*

"Captain," Z stood while addressing the Captain. "I'm not sure sending me with the soldiers who have the least amount of training is the correct move."

"Hey," Max interjected. "Who are you calling untrained? I promise you this, old man. You're lucky to have me on your team. Two reasons: first, I'd mop the floor with the rest of the team, excluding the Captain, of course. No offense, guys. Second, you'll want to be there to see the beating I throw down on this rogue once we locate him."

A small laugh rippled through the group at Max's self-assured banter before the Captain spoke up again.

"You do have Rodriguez, our weapon specialist, the doctor, your brainy companion Arcturus, and from my understanding, Miss Zoravic is a decent combatant these days. Apparently, nothing near the likes of young Rodriguez here, but still a very worthy ally to have," Captain Zephyr said. Lena nodded her head to the Captain in a show of thanks for noticing the hard work she'd been putting in.

"I think the teams are good as is. When we hit the ground, each of you needs to follow the orders of your leader. We are here for one reason: to get out there and find out anything we can about the location of this rogue Stellarnaut. I would like to have him dealt with by morning."

"Do you not think that is asking a bit much, Captain?" Ava asked.

"I do not," the Captain replied. "We are the Stellarnauts of the Ascendant 4, the greatest fleet in the galaxy. Bringing one man to justice in a single night doesn't seem to be too much to ask. Can I get a hoo-rah?"

"Hoo-rah!" Everyone except Arcturus and Z chimed in unison. The entire cabin nearly imploded from the resounding cheer of the seven Stellarnaut soldiers who participated.

The ship's hatch opened, and the crew exited through it. Lena stood on the landing pad and looked around. The buildings were huge, beyond anything she could have ever imagined. The night sky was outlined with building after building as far as her eyes could see. As she spun around in a circular fashion, there wasn't any sort of structure lit up like the festive tree her mother would set up for the winter solstice, blocking the horizon.

"Zoravic!" Z yelled. "Pay attention. We have a very important task ahead of us. Can't have you off in La La Land."

Lena turned back to the group, all of whom were looking at her. "I'm sorry," she said, her face tinged with red. "I've never seen anything like this before."

"It's not all it's cracked up to be," Max said. "One city is just as trashy as the next. You'll see soon enough, Lena. And this city is the worst in the galaxy."

"Come on, let's go," Z said. "Rodriguez, you lead. I will bring up the rear. Zoravic, you stay between Arcturus and Kim. Keep your eyes peeled for any unusual activity."

Lena was tired of being treated like a child, like the little sister everyone needed to protect.

"Why do I have to be in the center?" she demanded. "Why can't I take the lead or bring up the rear?"

"It's simple," Arcturus said. "You are the least trained and the most likely to lead us astray. Or, if you aren't watching closely, then someone from the rear will sneak up on you. Don't take it personally, Lena. Lieutenant Z is merely looking out for what's best for the team."

Lena hung her head. If Arcturus wasn't siding with her on this, there was no way she'd be able to convince any of the others that she was ready for more responsibility.

The group headed into the city, and Lena kept an eye out for anything she thought would lead them to either the rogue Stellarnaut or Blackwood. She knew the rogue was their number one priority, but, in her mind, her number one priority was Blackwood. If he was here, she intended to find him and get the revenge her family and she deserved. She was more determined than ever, and perhaps it was a little distracting for her because that was one of the main reasons she hopped on this space journey with them.

Once they made it off the landing pads and onto the city streets, she couldn't believe the number of people there. *"How could so many people physically live in such a small area?"* she asked herself.

Max led them through the streets as if he knew the right places to go, following the street signs and walking along the edge of the street to avoid ground-level vehicles. This was something Lena hadn't seen much of in her life on Zorath. She didn't understand how people navigated these streets without running into or over others; there were so many people. Maybe Z was correct in not putting her in a lead role.

They stopped, and Z was talking to some people while the rest of the group lingered, watching everyone else's movements. He asked about any other Stellarnauts, and they pointed them to a building a few blocks down the street.

"They said they've seen a Stellarnaut soldier here earlier," Z said when he returned to the group. "There's a club just down the street that he's frequented in the past few days."

Max headed that way, and the rest followed. After a brief walk, they entered the building.

It was loud inside, and there were so many people. The patrons of this club either danced and jumped around or sat around the outer perimeter, drinking alcoholic beverages and conversing with each other.

"We need to separate," Max said. "Spread through the club, mingle, listen, ask questions; we need to find out when he was last here and where he may have gone."

The group split up, each member going their own way, except for Lena and Arcturus, who stayed together. Lena led the way to the right, with Arcturus following closely behind her.

Max went left, while Z and Samuel went up to the center. As Lena walked among the tables, she heard someone say, "Hey, Mouse, over here."

Arcturus nudged Lena, whispering, "Did you hear…"

"Yes," she replied before he could finish his question. Lena was already looking in the direction of the voice. "Be quiet so I can hear what they're saying."

"Hey," a small woman with an elongated nose said.

*This must be Mouse,* Lena thought.

The woman's appearance couldn't be coincidental. "Do you have everything in order?"

"Yes, you and your boss should have all the Spectre ships he ordered by morning, and we'll get you cleared to leave as soon as they're loaded," the original speaker said.

"Good, we need to get off this rock," Mouse said. "That guy who killed Crusher, for some reason, is still hunting for us. We need to watch out for him."

"Yeah, I heard about that," the other person said. "She was a good pilot and a good friend. Hated to hear the news of her being shot down."

"We've recruited more people," Mouse said. "People come, and people go. Crusher was a good pilot and a friend. But, personally, I think her relationship with Black was getting in the way anyway."

"I don't know all the ins and outs of your crew," the other person said. "Either way, y'all meet me and Dodge on pad 96. We'll get you the rest of your Spectres and see you all safely off the planet."

"Will do," Mouse said. "And hey, thank you so much for pushing this order to the top of the list. I'm not completely sure what's up with the guy who killed Crusher, but he seems to have it out for us in a bad way." With that, she turned and walked away from the club.

Lena turned to Arcturus. "I'm going to follow her. She'll lead us to Blackwood, I'm sure of it."

"We should alert the others," Arcturus said.

"There's no time," Lena said urgently. "We'll lose her if we don't go now. There are too many people here. If I take my eyes off her, she'll be gone."

"Keep a connection with my life force," Arcturus said. "I will find you. I must get Max Rodriguez to come help you."

"I don't need Max for this. Blackwood is mine. No one will take him down except for me. This one is not business. It is personal," Lena asserted.

"If it is all the same to you, Lena," Arcturus said calmly. "Please keep the connection. I want to make sure everyone stays safe, especially you. Don't get too emotionally involved because you could get hurt. I understand you want to take out Blackwood, but not at the expense of your own safety."

"What else do I have, Arcturus? Everyone I love so dearly is gone! What good is living without them?"

"You're forgetting something...rather some other loved ones."

"Who am I missing? Everyone I love is gone!"

"Not everyone, Lena."

"I don't know what you mean?"

"Just look around. We love you too."

"Oh my! I am touched! I love you all, too."

"Isn't that enough for you then, Lena?"

"It is more than enough. I am sorry if I hurt your feelings, Arcturus. I did not mean what I said to undermine you all and whatever everyone has done for me. It means a lot, honestly."

"It means a lot to us too, honestly, especially me."

"Awww!"

Lena reached out with her mind, pulling ever so slightly on Arcturus's life force, just enough to feel his presence without draining his energy too much. She followed the petite woman from the club. Mouse was the perfect call sign for this woman; not only did her appearance fit the moniker, but she could also nose her way through a crowd with the agility of a mouse navigating through boxes and canned food in a cupboard.

Lena stayed far enough back so she wouldn't be noticed but had to stay close enough that she wouldn't lose Mouse in the crowd. Mouse, being small and nimble, was able to navigate the crowd with ease, while Lena was completely decked out in her Zephyr suit. It wasn't as bulky as some other suits she'd seen, but her suit wasn't exactly the sleek third-generation suit the rest of her crew wore. She had a harder time making her way through the crowds, but she didn't let the smaller woman elude her.

Mouse turned down an alley, causing Lena to stop and peer around the corner. When she stuck her head around the corner, she was met with a pipe to the front of her helmet. She was knocked from her feet, and she could hear the sound of feet running away from her.

"Stay away from me, you crazy bastard," Mouse screamed over her shoulder.

Reaching out, Lena could still feel her connection with Arcturus. She was afraid the blow to her face would cause her to lose it, but the energy was still coming to her, so she got to her feet and ran after the small woman. Her cover had been blown; there was no need to try to stay stealthy any longer.

Mouse lived up to her nickname once again. She ran through the streets and evaded vehicles and people as if she were a small mouse fleeing from the black cat back in her father's garage. She scurried up and over a fence. Mouse slid feet first under another fence around the next corner.

All the while, Lena had to use the abilities of her suit to help her leap the fences or just blow right through the locks on the gates. The longer the chase went on, the harder Lena pushed herself and pulled upon the suit's ability to keep her moving. This was

Blackwood's crew member; she couldn't lose her. She wouldn't lose her. The sake of her family's revenge was at stake here.

Lena ran harder and faster than she ever thought possible. If it hadn't been for all those years training her mind and body, there's no way she would have been able to keep up with this elusive woman. Mouse rounded a corner just as Lena was about to grab her. Lena activated the thrusters on the palm of her hands, allowing her to round the corner without having to swing too wide. This gave her the advantage she needed to end this cat-and-mouse chase. Lena reached out and dove forward, grappling Mouse from behind and taking her to the ground.

Mouse held up her arms and said, "Don't kill me, I'm just..."

Lena cut her off. "I'm not going to kill you," she said. *Not yet, anyway,* she thought. "I just need to know where to find Blackwood."

"Blackwood?" Mouse asked, confusion evident on her face. "You mean Black?"

"I mean Jaxson Blackwood," Lena clarified. "Your boss, your Captain. You must tell me. I have unfinished business with him."

Mouse shook her head, the confusion on her face growing even more pronounced. "Yeah, Black. He hasn't used the name Blackwood for nearly thirty years now," Mouse explained. "How do you know that name?"

"Where is he?" Lena demanded.

"I can't take you to Black," Mouse replied as she got to her feet and dusted herself off.

"You're not who I thought you were, anyway. You're a regular Stellarnaut. You can't hurt me."

"Who were you expecting?" Lena asked, exactly knowing who she was talking about.

"Another Stellarnaut," Mouse said. "He's dressed like you but much larger, and I'd be dead right now. He's been tracking us for a while. If I do take you to Black, maybe you could help get this other Stellarnaut off our backs so we can get back to business. Do we have a deal?"

"I'm looking for the Stellarnaut too, not just Blackwood," Lena admitted. "If you bring me to Blackwood, I'll help get the Stellarnaut off your back. You'll lose your boss, but you won't have to worry about the Stellarnaut any longer. Now, do we have a deal?"

Mouse stood there, gawking at Lena. Her eyes widened as she spoke, "If you take Black, I would be the leader. Everyone would have to answer to me. This would be huge for me!"

"I don't care what you do with Blackwood's crew. It's none of my business," Lena replied. "I just want him, and we'll deal with your Stellarnaut problem. Do we have a deal?"

Mouse looked at Lena, fear evident in her eyes once again. "Wait a minute. Let me understand one thing, please. What did he ever do to you? Why do you want him so badly?"

Tears welled in Lena's eyes, and she couldn't control them. "That's my concern. He'll know why as soon as he sees me. It is better you do not get involved with this. Once you bring me to him, the truth shall set you free."

Arcturus rounded the corner with Max right behind him. "Lena, what's going on?" Max asked. "Arcturus said you found someone and needed help."

"I caught her," Lena explained. "She's going to lead us straight to Blackwood. She's his..." Lena paused, unsure of Mouse's role in the crew.

"I'm Mouse," Mouse interjected, standing as tall as she could. "I pilot Black's **Odyssey**, and I am also the head of communications for the crew."

"I don't care who you are and what you do," Max stated. "How does this help us with the rogue Stellarnaut, Lena?"

"He's tracking Blackwood, too," Lena replied. "If we find Blackwood, we're bound to find the rogue too. We can kill two birds with one stone, in fact, rather two rogues."

"Lena has an excellent plan," Arcturus added.

"We'll look into it," Max agreed. "Why are you going to bring us to your boss? What did Lena promise you? What deals are you guys making here without my knowledge?"

"She told me she wouldn't kill me and that I could be the new leader," Mouse answered.

Max laughed, "You're learning, Zoravic."

Mouse looked at Lena and mouthed the word "Zoravic," then paused briefly before mouthing the word "shit." She took a deep breath.

"Follow me; I'll take you all to our base," Mouse said. "The only thing I ask is that you don't destroy any of our Spectres and that you don't interfere with me departing the planet in the morning. Now, do we all have a deal?"

"Deal," Max interjected before Lena could speak up. "We'll need to hide out in your shop while we wait for this rogue Stellarnaut to come for you. If you help us, we will help you."

Mouse just shrugged and replied, "Okay," then turned and led them back the way they came. She glanced over her shoulder at Lena. "I was trying to lead you away from the base. I thought I was about to lose you when I rounded that corner. I didn't think you'd be able to cut that corner like that with all that gear on. How did you get around it so fast, anyhow?"

As they walked another block, Mouse turned up another alley. "My suit helps a lot more than it hinders. You'd be surprised," Lena explained.

"Don't tell her too much about the suits," Max cautioned.

"We know a lot about your suits already," Mouse said. "Black actually used to have one. He may still have it, but he was never able to power it up. I could never understand why that was so.." She glanced back at Lena again before swaying the next part. "We actually nearly found a power source strong enough to power it, but when we went back, we never could find it. We scoured that planet for months with no luck at all."

"How in the hell did he get his hands on a Zephyr suit?" Max asked. "You have to go through extreme training to become a Stellarnaut. Even if he found an old suit, if his DNA isn't linked to the suit, he couldn't use it anyway."

Mouse laughed, "He's a fool. He's spent most of his life trying to find a way to power that suit, and you're telling me he couldn't use it anyway?" She laughed so hard that she had to stop for a minute. "Woo, that's hilarious," she said. She stopped laughing and said, "What's that say about me? I've been following the fool for years." Mouse shook her head and then continued down the alley.

"How far out is it?" Lena asked.

"Just a few more blocks," Mouse replied.

"I think someone is following us; be careful and watch your steps," Arcturus noted.

Mouse looked around. There were some people walking past the end of the alley. Another person was relieving themselves at the end of a dumpster. "It's probably nothing," she said. "There are so many people walking around on this planet; it always makes you feel like you're being followed. It's right over here."

She turned to face a door, her hands moving across a keypad on the door handle. After a few seconds, the door opened, and she stepped inside. Lena followed right behind her, with Max and Arcturus close behind.

"Mouse, welcome ba..." a voice started as they entered the building. The voice was familiar to Lena, but it was broken. She looked at the man who'd started speaking. He had a hood over his head, and scars ran down his face. The face was older, but there was no denying it. After all these years, she was looking into the eyes of the man who killed her family once again. Lena's jaw dropped!

# Chapter 19

Voltorin

6558 ASST

Max stepped forward, removing his helmet. His face bore a stern and angry expression.

"Ah, Maxwell," Blackwood greeted. "And here I was thinking this had to do with something else. I am sorry about Maria's death and would like you to know about it. I had nothing to do with it whatsoever, contrary to what you believe."

"No?" Max said. "Then why hasn't her killer been dealt with? Why are you planning on fleeing the planet, knowing very well that he's still here?"

"Maxwell, please, calm yourself," Blackwood said in a soft and comforting tone. "If I had any idea where this phantom, this rogue Stellarnaut, was, do you not think he would have been dealt with already? I would have been the first to take him out and..."

Lena stepped up next to Max, her hand resting on the revolver at her side. She whispered, "I'm going to take him out now."

Max turned to her sharply, "No, we're using him as a pawn. You can't have him until we lure in the rogue. Hold your horses, please!"

Lena pulled Max's face around so he was looking at her. She opened the visor on her helmet, revealing red eyes and tears streaming down her face. "Max," Lena pleaded with him in a hushed voice. "He killed my family. You have no idea how long I have been waiting for this, and you are asking me to wait! Are you kidding me!"

"Who do we have here, Maxwell?" Blackwood inquired.

"Don't worry about it," Max dismissed. "You'll learn her identity soon enough. For now, I need to know where the rogue Stellarnaut is. He's the one who killed Maria, and I want him dead."

"Maxwell, I've told you to calm yourself. I want the same person, too. We will find him," Blackwood urged.

"I'm not Maria. If you tell me to calm myself one more time, I'll end you right now. Believe me when I tell you, I won't even hesitate," Max warned. "His location, now." Max's voice was elevated at this point.

"What makes you think I know where he is?" Blackwood asked.

"Because I know you," Max retorted. "Take me to him, and then I'll leave you to my friend here. I believe that the both of you have some unfinished business to take care of!"

Blackwood glanced at Lena. "This little thing, she doesn't seem like she'll be too hard to handle despite what she may think. I have handled way bigger obstacles than her. Now, the only way I'll tell you is if you promise once I do, you're out of my hair."

"I promise," Max affirmed. "You have my word. It will be you and Lena while I deal with the rogue. I won't be involved in that. That's not my rodeo, space cowboy!"

"Very well," Blackwood agreed. "I've paid some spies to track him down and follow him back to his hideout. His location is..."

"No, no, no," Max interjected. "You will take me to him."

"I hope you're as good as you think you are, kid," Blackwood said, wearing the same smirk he had the day Lena saw him on Zorath—the day he took everything from her. "If not, we're all dead. Follow me."

Lena's fingers continued to flick against the handle of the revolver at her side. Blackwood walked right in front of her, but she couldn't do anything about it because she had to hold up her end of the deal. She gets Blackwood; Max gets the rogue. They made the deal years ago, and she's never forgotten her end. It's actually happening; they'll both have their revenge before the night ends.

Blackwood led them down a busy street, and Lena kept a watchful eye. It seemed like Max and Arcturus were doing the same. As much as she wanted to help Max get his revenge, she would drop Blackwood where he stood if she got even the slightest hint of a trap.

"Where are you taking us?" Max asked.

"Do you really think I set up my base of operations in the same vicinity as the crazed maniac?" Blackwood retorted. "I hope you all didn't get too close to Mouse on your walk over. Because once I'm done with you," he motioned to Lena, "she's next. I can't believe that rat sold me out."

"Mouse intends to take over as crew leader once I finish with you," Lena countered.

"Ha, Mouse couldn't lead if she wanted to," Blackwood scoffed. "Hell, the only reason I let her stick around is because she's a pretty good pilot, and she follows orders better than most men I've worked with. Ahh, here we are. His hideout is right around here, according to my spies."

Max approached the door and knocked, but nothing happened. He knocked again, and then there was movement on the roof above the door. "There," Lena pointed as she spotted the silhouette of a Stellarnaut.

Max looked up and saw the figure. His suit was an older model like Lena's. Without hesitation, Max aimed his gun and fired. "Lena, Blackwood is yours. I'm going after the rogue." He dashed, grabbed the side of the building, and started climbing.

Lena watched him get a few feet up before she reached for the revolver from her hip. As she went to turn, Blackwood kicked her in the side, knocking her off balance. She nearly dropped the revolver but was able to activate the thruster in her palm, catching herself from falling.

Blackwood turned and charged at Arcturus and shouldered his way through the Biotan, knocking him to the ground. Arcturus was no longer a threat to him.

Max made it to the rooftop and was caught with a boot to the face. His helmet was still hanging on his hip, giving him no protection to his head. Max lost his footing and fell from the roof, crashing to the ground beside Lena. The entire team was unable to shake off Blackwood.

Lena spared him a glance before she pulled the gun out and fired it at the fleeing Blackwood. The echoing blast from the gun caused Blackwood to stop in his tracks and turn back, looking in Lena's direction. It seemed like Blackwood had met someone familiar. This was perhaps not the way he wanted this meeting to go about.

Blackwood looked straight at the weapon that made the sound. "My old gun, I know who you are. You're the pesky little brat that did this to me." He pulled back his hood and ran his fingers along the scars on his face. "I went back to that godforsaken planet a few years later. I thought maybe you died, the way you were laying there panting after you did, whatever it was you did to me. Glad you didn't. I've been looking forward to gunning you down like I did your mom for a long time now. You got me now. Go ahead! Hit me with your best shot, you amateur Stellarnaut!"

Lena tensed at the thought of what he'd done to her mother all those years ago. She readied herself to fire the next round; she'd been saving the four remaining bullets the gun had in it for Blackwood. This was the moment she had been waiting for so long. The time had finally come, and she was ready to fire. She planned on putting all four of them through his black heart, but three would do just as well. Just as she was about to pull the trigger, she said, "This is for…"

Before she could pull the trigger, something strange happened. Lena got hit from the side, knocking her across the street. She slammed against the wall of the building and fell to the ground. Looking up, she saw the rogue Stellarnaut standing there looking at Blackwood. His suit was exactly like hers, definitely a second-generation suit. The next moment would change her life forever. He turned his head to her and said, "You can't have him; that honor belongs to me. I have been waiting far too long for this, Lena."

Lena's eyes widened behind her visor. Tears began to well in them; she couldn't breathe.

She could not believe her eyes. *How could this man know my name?* She was shell-shocked! Her arms and legs were heavy; she couldn't move. Her body heaved uncontrollably because after all these years, the voice that just came from that man, the man she came here to help her friend kill, was one she would never forget as long as she lived. She mustered the will to lift her head, looked back up at that man, and said a single word, "Daddy."

# Epilogue

## Earth

## 6554 ASST

"Father, I bring news of Janus."

"Ahh, Orion, my son," Maximilian said, greeting his eldest son without even looking up from his work. It had been nearly two hundred years since Orion had laid eyes on his father, and the man looked the same as he did the last time he saw him. Maximilian Zephyr didn't look a day older than he did when he left Earth over six thousand years ago. "What has your brother gotten himself into now?"

Orion stepped closer to his father, who was standing at a computer. This computer was far superior to any computer in the galaxy. Maximilian Zephyr had designed and built it to help harness the ether-lumina he used to build and power his Stellarnaut Armada.

"Janus has made a move against the Intergalactic Star Fleet," Orion said. "He attacked and commandeered one of their ships off the planet Navaria."

"You traveled all the way to the Sol System to bring me news of dealings between your little brother and Krytus?" Maximilian asked.

"Father, Janus is in the wrong here. He attacked a Star-Fleet ship to protect a lesser species," Orion said. "His interference on

Navaria with Star-Fleet business could bring trouble to the Armada, Father."

"What business does Krytus have on Navaria?" Maximilian asked. "The Navarians are a peaceful people who can't even leave their planet. I know Krytus already had dealings with them, and they didn't go his way. The Navarians failed as subjects for his experiments. They were not cut out for those."

"How do you know of that?" Orion asked.

"Orion, my son," Maximilian said. "I know more about what is happening in the galaxy than you would think I do. It is your job to police the galaxy; it is my job to know what is going on in the galaxy."

Orion looked over at Maximilian's lab assistant. "Do you know it is rumored that Janus has a Biotan aboard his ship?"

Maximilian looked at his son for the first time since he arrived at this news. "These rumors are false, Orion," he spat back. "There has not been a Biotan surface in over three thousand years. If your brother has a Biotan, I would have heard of it. I have no knowledge of such an occurrence at all."

Orion knew that would get his father's attention. He needed permission from his father to track down his brother and handle the situation between him and Kraytus. He couldn't let the Stellarnauts go to war with the Intergalactic Star-Fleet. It would ruin all the work he had done for over a millennium.

"Janus's crew is loyal," Orion said. "Their loyalty is to him, not the Armada. Something must be done. Let's go speak with Krytus. Have him call off his soldiers and put an end to a war before it starts. I will bring Janus in myself."

"I can't leave," Maximilian said. "There is still much that must be done here."

"Father, this world is dead," Orion gestured around. "This laboratory is the only thing left here that is worth saving. Why do you insist on staying here? You can't save this world. No one can!"

"Xylar," Maximilian said.

"Yes, Maximilian," Xylar, the Biotan assistant whom Orion had glanced at before making his claim about the Biotan aboard Janis's ship.

"Will you please explain to my son why we must stay here?" Maximilian asked.

"Absolutely," Xylar responded. "Orion Zephyr, Maximilian, and I are working towards a greater future for our galaxy. We are currently obtaining enough ether-lumina to sustain the current Stellarnaut Armada. This is through my people, whom we have currently sedated in this laboratory. However, we would like to expand the Armada by double in the next two thousand years. It is impossible to do so with the current output of energy."

"Oh yeah," Orion interrupted. "And just how do you plan on doing that?"

"I am certain that you noticed Sol before you entered the atmosphere. On this planet, there were schematics for building a Dyson sphere," Xylar said. "A device unattainable with the world's technology and resources when designed. Between Maximilian's intelligence combined with my own, we were able to use this world's resources, along with the resources of surrounding planets, to start construction on the sphere. The sphere, if built correctly, should be able to harness enough energy from Sol to power an armada three times the size of the current one for more than ten thousand years. This would also allow us to cease operations on the current method of obtaining ether-lumina."

"I am currently more than two-thirds of the way through building the Dyson sphere, son," Maximilian said. "Therefore, I do not have time to go off and try to save your brother from a war with my old Conrad. If you feel that your brother should be saved from Kraytus's fleet, travel to whatever part of the galaxy Krytus has on his Titan ship and speak to him yourself. Or better yet, if you feel it is a better alternative, go hunt down your brother and deal with him. Then, by all means, do that; just leave me to do my work."

"Very well," Orion said. "Thank you, Father. I will travel on behalf of the Stellarnauts to deal with the situation."

"If your brother does have a Biotan aboard his ship, I would very much like you to return here with it in your custody." Maximilian looked back at his computer. "I built the Stellarnaut Armada to police the galaxy and put my children at the helm of their own ships so I wouldn't have to deal with the problems of the galaxy. Don't bring them to me anymore."

Orion turned and walked from his father's lab. He had no intentions of seeking out Kraytus Sivik; he already knew where he was and where he stood in this situation. Orion had been dealing with the Intergalactic Star-Fleet for years, with Kraytus Sivik more specifically. The Star-Fleet leader promised to give Orion the same enhancements he had given himself if he convinced his siblings to join forces with them. Sivik wanted nothing more than to take down Maximilian Zephyr and seize control of the Stellarnauts.

Maximilian, standing there watching his eldest son leave, reached out with his mind and grabbed one of the panels that lay on the ground to the left. The panel was lifted from its position and floated across the room, butted up against another panel. He then shot an electrical current from his fingertip and fused the panels together; then, another one was lifted and moved in the same direction.

"I hope my children can manage the galaxy until we have harnessed the power of Sol," Maximilian said to his companion, Xylar.

"As do I, sir," Xylar responded. "We will need every Biotan we have when it comes time to fulfill our destiny. The time is not far, and we shall get to it soon enough."

Made in the USA
Columbia, SC
04 January 2025

48763808R00133